Perfectly Reasonable

RACHEL RAFFERTY

.

Perfectly Reasonable

Published by Rachel Rafferty 2022

Copyright © 2022 Rachel Rafferty
Print Edition

Visit: Rachelrafferty.com

'How About I Be Me'

Sinéad O'Connor
(I'm Not Bossy, I'm the Boss)

Prologue

IN MY OPINION, they were more periwinkle than purple. But, of course, the exact shade was irrelevant. It only mattered that they were evident. And they were, clear as day—those two elegant, straight lines that were going to change my life forever.

Before breaking the news to Declan, I searched for my mother's diary that she'd kept when she was expecting me. I found the section where she wrote about being pregnant. She used phrases like '*long awaited*', '*much wanted*' and '*over the moon*'. I traced my finger over her handwritten words in an attempt to feel her presence. I wanted to share my joy with her, but my phone rang, disturbing our connection.

'Declan.'

'Oh, sorry. Are you in the middle of something? I just wondered how you got on this morning. Any news?' he asked.

I looked down once more at my mother's pages. I loved her handwriting. She never looped the tall letters; only the long, below-the-line letters such as g, j and y were circularly curved. The tall ones like b, d, h, k and l were skinny, single lines, veering ever so slightly to the right. I tried and failed on many occasions to emulate her penmanship.

'Cara? Are you still there?' Declan asked.

A sort of sadness befell me that she wouldn't be around to support me at this special time of my life. I froze when I remembered how she used to drop subtle hints about wanting to be a young granny, so she'd be able to enjoy her grandchildren.

'Was it negative again, Cara? Ah no, not again. We really thought this time was different. You said it yourself. You felt different.'

'Declan, wait,' I answered.

I looked once more at the open diary in front of me and one particular entry caught my eye. It was dated December 14th, 1977.

'Josie in the office asked if I was pregnant. She only wants to give her sister-in-law my job, so I told her no. I said I'd just put on a bit of weight since buying Delia Smith's latest cookery book. There was no way I was telling that office gossip. *Always tell a lie when the truth doesn't fit in,* so that's what I did. I want to hold on to my job as long as possible to make sure my baby gets the best of everything.'

It made me smile—*always tell a lie when the truth doesn't fit in.*

'Are you okay, Cara?'

'Sorry, Declan. It's just … It's just, I didn't do the test yet. I think I'll wait until you get home from work. We'll do it together.'

I'd destroy the periwinkle lined one and we could share the moment later on. I was doing this for him. In the meantime, I read a few more pages of my mother's wisdom before driving to Stylemama. No bump yet obviously, but no harm in browsing.

Later that evening, I knew I'd done the right thing when I saw Declan's face light up.

'We did it, Cara!' he exclaimed. 'We finally did it!'

'I know, Declan, I did!' I said, matching his elation. 'I did it!'

As he embraced me, he whispered in my ear.

'Can't believe it! Are we really going to have a baby? Is this really happening?'

'Yes! Yes, it is! I'm really going to have a baby! It's finally happening, Declan! I'm pregnant!'

He welled up and smiled. 'We are. We really are.'

Chapter One

(Almost six years later)

I DROPPED TO my knees in the driveway. I couldn't help it. I raised my gaze skyward, together with a clenched fist.

'How could she? How could she do this to me?'

I'd never questioned Lucy's motives up to now. Never had reason to. Hardly a cross word had exchanged between us, which made this rejection harder to swallow. It was a betrayal. She had vehemently denied my existence and showed no remorse.

'After all I've done for you ... Et tu, Lucy?' I looked heavenward and pleaded into the early morning Dublin sky.

And SHE knew! She knew what a monumental day this was! She was aware of the extent to which I'd been dreading this day. Yet, when push came to shove, she simply wouldn't play ball. I began muttering to myself in the driveway.

'That's what I get, is it? That's all I get for my blood, sweat and tears over the past five years?!'

I admit it. I lost it, right there and then. Thank goodness, no one in Cedarwood Drive seemed to be up early enough to witness my outburst on this crisp, blue-skied, sunny Monday morning in September. It was the day I was returning to work, after a five-year career break. I'd imagined myself swanning into the office looking refreshed and glowing, sharing my newfound motherly wisdom with my wide-eyed, envious colleagues. But now, because of Lucy's morning antics, I'd be tumbling into the office in a heap of tears and dejection.

In Lucy's paltry five years on this earth, she had been a model child. That's what made my humiliation cut so deep. It was new, unexpected and raw. And it was happening right now in our new childminder's front garden.

I paused and considered the series of events that occured in the last half hour. Lucy had been busy playing with the other children when I approached to say goodbye. My darling daughter didn't wave or answer my 'toodeloos'. She didn't even turn around. Our new childminder, Emma, tried to reassure me that this was normal and even a good thing, that Lucy was too preoccupied to bid farewell, but I was having none of it. I stood, waiting, welling up for at least ten minutes, but no joy. Lucy was content to ignore me and carry on serving her new friends tea from a cheap, plastic, chipped tea set.

I turned to Emma. 'Five years. Five years of my life I gave that child. I dedicated every second, minute, hour, day, week, month and year to her. I mean 24/7 and THIS is what I get!'

'Ah look, Cara, she's happy to be here. Isn't that much better than her crying or clinging to you and not letting you go to work?'

'Emma, all I'm asking for is a show of emotion! Maybe a little affection? Christ, I'd be happy now if she just looked my way! It's like she's forgotten me already! When I think of all those special times we shared together. None of it matters now that she's got some new buddies and a rake of Ikea children's toys to play with!'

Emma walked away looking exasperated at this point, but I remained exactly where I was. Surely, Lucy would dash over at any second and hug me and tell me how much she loved me. Then, she would jump up and wrap her little legs around me, clinging to me, crying, '*no*'. She would say, '*No, Mommy, you can't go to work and leave me here with these strangers! What about our mommy/daughter days out, our babyccinos, girly movies and finger painting? No, Mommy, I command that you stay at home with me! I'll scream and scream and scream if you leave to go to work!*' However, she didn't say any of those things. She stayed without protest and played happily.

When Emma called them into the kitchen for

breakfast, little Lucy left the playroom without a backward glance. I was left alone. I didn't know what to do with myself, so I turned my critical eye to Emma's choice of furniture, carpet and artwork on the walls. Far be it from me to be judgemental, but after a quick scan I couldn't escape the fact that I disapproved of almost everything. With that, I promptly followed the children to the kitchen. I peered in through the open door. Well ... everything looked just fine and dandy in the kitchen, which sickened me to the core. All the children were wearing bibs to protect their school uniforms and everyone seemed to be following Emma's instructions to a T. They were laughing and talking while they ate. My huffing and puffing must have been overheard by Emma.

'Cara, honestly, everything is fine here. We'll be leaving for school in half an hour. I don't want you to be late for your first day back at work. Really, it's okay. You can go.'

'I just want to wait here and make sure Lucy doesn't throw up her breakfast, because she knows I'm going back to work today. You know what they say about young children carrying all their angst in their tummies. She's hiding it well now, but she's actually tied up in knots about me returning to work. She's probably too embarrassed to let it all out in front of her new friends, but ...'

'Cara, if you don't mind, I think it's better that

you go now while they're all settled. In a few minutes they'll be dashing to the bathroom to brush teeth and looking for coats and you'll ... well, I'm sorry to say it, but you'll be in the way.'

Oh, I knew she was right. Of course she was. I tiptoed to the breakfast table. 'G...g...goodbye, L...Lucy, darling,' I stammered, as if addressing royalty. The children chuckled together when young Sam did an impression of his hero, Fireman Sam. My heart sank when Lucy threw her head back and laughed the loudest.

That was when Emma led me to the front door and into the garden. This was when my legs gave way. My knees dug into the pebbles in the driveway. Honestly, I didn't even notice the blood seeping through the newly born rip in my tights. The only pain I felt was deep in my heart. The separation anxiety was a one-way street. I heard Emma closing the front door, leaving me alone in my suffering. Alone, and on my knees. The tears streamed down my face, along with thick, heavy, black streaks of mascara. I was so lost in my anguish that I didn't hear my neighbour Bernadette approaching.

'Ah Cara, is today the day?'

I got the fright of my life and pulled myself up.

'Oh, hi Bernadette. Yes, yes, today's the day. I'm due in the office in half an hour. My first day back in over five years! You know, when you add in the extended maternity leave and ...'

'Ah, God love you. Best of luck. Don't worry about little Lucy. She'll be grand. Emma's brilliant. All the kids love her! There's a waiting list of children around here only dying to get in there. *"The House of Fun"*, they call it! Hahaha!'

Well, that certainly didn't make me feel any better, but I faked a smile anyway. Lucy had loved being at home with Mommy. She'd loved the regimented routines we'd stuck to every day. Swimming on Mondays, art on Tuesdays, visiting Granny on Wednesdays, shopping on Thursdays, movies on Fridays and cheering on Daddy at his GAA matches every Saturday and Sunday. None of these beloved activities would be achievable anymore, what with my new demanding work schedule.

Bernadette bid farewell and went on her merry way, while I wiped the streaming mascara from my cheeks. I manifested just enough energy to get into my car to drive to Crawford's Recruitment Agency for my first day back.

✧   ✧   ✧

ON MY WAY, I thought about how the family schedule would have to change. Let's see ... If I prioritised the absolute necessities, like art and crafts, Lucy's babyccino and visiting Granny, it'd give me clarity on what I can scrap. Oh gosh, I reflected, it looked like Declan's weekend matches would have to take the hit. He'd understand. He'd have to. He was used to me skipping the odd match here and there anyway, when the phantom PMS would strike, approximately one hour pre match time. Purely coincidental, of course. Us mortals can't control these things. If truth be told though, after our eight years of married life, I'd never managed to foster Declan's love of GAA. I actually hated traipsing along to the matches every weekend, but all the WAGs seemed to do it, so I felt obliged.

Yes, from now on, I'd be delighted to rearrange the schedule and slip in a Saturday afternoon of leisurely shopping and babyccinos, rather than standing on the sidelines in the freezing cold, cheering on my husband. I was beginning to see the positives of going back to work, but they were few and far between.

I wondered, though, if Declan might hop on the schedule change and wonder why the PMS wouldn't stop me from going shopping on a Saturday, when it had so often prevented me from attending his matches. I'd have to assert that the shopping simply had to be done regardless. There was no getting away from it. We needed food to eat and clothes to wear. And of course, Lucy loved her babyccinos in the coffee shop every Thursday with Mommy, so we would uphold this tradition for Lucy's sake, but do it on a Saturday from now on. Ah yes, back to work, back to the grind, but every cloud and all that...

✧ ✧ ✧

THE TALL, OMINOUS building that housed Crawford's Recruitment Agency loomed before me. I parked in what seemed to be the very last parking space. That was strange—I didn't think I was late. Had they taken on extra staff since I last worked here, over five years ago? Apart from the packed car park, not much else had changed. The grey walls were still grey, the mat gathered in the revolving entrance door as it always did, and the lift was surprisingly slower than one would think it should be. Really, I remembered it was slow, I expected it to be slow, yet it amazed me how slow it actually was.

I was a jittery wreck pushing in the door to my open-plan office. It felt like such a long time since I'd been there. It was. And since Lucy was born, I didn't make much effort to remain in touch. That said, neither did they.

'Welcome back, Cara! It's great to see you! How's Lucy getting on with her new minder?' my boss, Barbara, enquired. At that exact moment, an invisible wall erected itself between me and

Barbara. I could see the transparent blocks stacking up around me, only I wished it was real. I wished Barbara could see it too, so she'd know she couldn't penetrate me. I was no longer defenceless. No more was I prepared to be her wrecking ball, as I had been in the olden days. I was a mother. I had purpose in my life. I wasn't striving to keep up with my peers, because I was one of them now. Successfully married and proud mother to a darling little girl. I would cling to that. At last, I had something to cling to. It felt like protection.

'Oh well, she was very emotional saying goodbye to me this morning. Her minder had to drag her off me. It was pretty brutal, to be honest.' I bent the truth ever so slightly. As my mother used to say, '*Always tell a lie when the truth doesn't fit in*'. I hung on to this like a life motto. 'Yes, Barbara, it might be hard for me to peel her off me in the mornings, so don't be shocked if I'm a few minutes late every now and then.'

'Oh, of course, Cara. That's to be expected in the initial stages. And don't worry, hon, we've all been there.'

'Thanks, Barbara, thanks for that,' I said, as I wiped a tear from my eye on my way to my desk. As I turned my head, I clocked Barbara and Kate raising their eyes in mutual fake sympathy. Oh, there they go again. They're still like that. They haven't changed. I despaired at the thought.

Five o'clock came and went. I made numerous attempts to leave, but a call came through or a folder was dropped on my desk. At five thirty-three, I bumped into Barbara on her way out the door.

'Well done, Cara! You survived your first day back to the grind! Things have changed around here, haven't they?'

'Well, yes, I didn't expect to be so busy on my first day back. You know, I thought I could ease back into it, but I barely had time to take a lunch break.'

'I hear you, hon. It's been mad busy like this for nearly two years now, with no let up. We've actually changed our start time to 8.30am, just to make sure we're outta here by 5.30. I didn't want to alarm you on your first day back, but you were a half-hour late, hon.'

'Eight-thirty am! That means dropping Lucy to the minder at 7.30! I don't even know if she's open then!'

'Oh, what about Declan? Couldn't he drop her at eight, instead of you? I'm sure with his handy car services job, he has a bit of flexibility. I mean how else would he fit in all his Gaelic training, hahaha!'

'Em, it's just that I'm the one Lucy relies on. I help get her settled in the minder's, do her pigtails and find her teddy and ...'

'Don't stress, Cara. Tell Declan that he'll have to do all that from now on. Write him a list. I do it for my Joe and he got the hang of things, no problem.'

'But you don't understand, you see I …'

'No buts, Cara. I need you here at 8.30. Write a list of morning requirements for Declan and get him to do the drop-off. I'm sure he'll agree, it's a perfectly reasonable request.'

Chapter Two

A S SOON AS Lucy went to bed that evening, I decided to share the new family schedule with Declan. We sat down together on the chesterfield, and I laid out tea and biscuits on the marble, rose gold coffee table. A piece of bespoke, designer furniture that was dear to my heart. Declan had no idea how much it cost. He didn't tend to exhibit much interest in the price of items, until he found out the actual price of the item. Occasionally I'd let it slip, but usually by then, it was too late for returns.

'What?' Declan asked. 'You're not coming to any more of my matches? But Lucy loves watching me play! You can't take that away from her, just because you're going back to work!'

I'd more or less expected this reaction, so I was prepared. 'I'm not taking anything away from her. You can still play GAA out the back garden together!'

'It's not called playing GAA! It's Gaelic, Cara! I play Gaelic football and have done since I was a chiseler. And ever since we had our first date ten years ago! You should know that by now!'

'Well, whatever! You can still share your skills with Lucy in the back garden and she won't miss out.' I attempted to sound reassuring.

'Share my skills! Share my skills! That's not why I want you both there at the matches! I want you to absorb the atmosphere and get carried away with the excitement. I'm not trying to coach both of you, y'know!'

'Look Declan, Granny needs her weekly visit. It's important to her that she sees Lucy regularly and she can't drive, so she can't come to us. And every normal working family does their weekly shop on a Saturday, and yes, it takes half the day to do it properly. I have to go around the world to make sure I get the best of everything for our family's nutritional needs. Dunnes for the staples, Staffords for the bread, Brady's Butcher for the meat and Market Fresh for the fruit and veg.'

He wasn't having it. 'Yeah, you say that, but doesn't your best friend, Beatrice, live near Dunnes? Your favourite coffee shop is beside the bakery. You fancy the pants off the butcher and there's a playground around the corner from Market Fresh! See, I know the real reasons why you have to make a day of it. You could easily head up to Lidl or Aldi and get everything we need for half the price!'

'How dare you! I only buy the best, premium ingredients to feed our family and you know it!'

With that, I snapped up the remote control and switched on the nine o'clock news. After Declan's extended protest, we'd missed half of it already and there was no way in hell I was going to miss the weather forecast too.

✧　　✧　　✧

A FEW DAYS later, I overheard Declan venting his frustrations on the phone with his friend Jim.

'It's a joke, Jim. She has me dropping off Lucy Monday to Friday and collecting her two days a week! I have to miss my Wednesday night coaching session. She's treating me like a doormat, now that she's back at work.'

Declan was scraping his mucky football boots in the utility room, as he chatted to Jim on loudspeaker. He didn't even try to be discreet. I stopped at the door without being noticed, to listen to Jim's response.

'You see, Declan, I tried to explain to you at the time. She's not one of us. She has zero interest in Gaelic football and doesn't seem to understand what a pivotal role it plays in our lives. She doesn't get it, and never did!'

'But Jim, d'you remember, she used to come to all my matches in the good ole days, d'you remember that?'

'Ah Declan, that was just to win you over. Sure, don't they all do that! Keith's wife, Jane, used to pretend she was a Liverpool supporter until that ring was on her finger. The problem with your Cara was that everyone else could see through her, except you.'

'And now she's keeping Lucy from coming along to the Saturday matches to support me. Bringing her out for a babyccino instead! Sure, Lucy grew outta them years ago! She'd much rather puck around with a hurl and play with the other kids at the pitch. But Cara won't have it, there's no talking to her.'

'She's her own woman, that's for sure. Pints tomorrow night, Declan?'

'Yeah, go on. Sure, why not?'

That's when I left. I'd heard enough.

✧   ✧   ✧

THE FOLLOWING EVENING when Declan arrived home late, I got the whiff of Guinness from him.

'How was work?' he asked, trying a bit too hard to be nonchalant.

'Declan, I hate being back. I knew after five years off it would be a shock to my system, but I didn't think things would change this much in the office. It's so corporate and hostile now. Everything has to be above board, which I like, but there's no leeway for error anymore. There's no friendliness or downtime. We're constantly on high alert. It's like I've been away too long and can't seem to catch up with everyone else.'

'Ah, that's terrible, love. Is there any way you could switch to a four-day week, or even part time?'

'No, I asked about reducing my hours and Barbara laughed at me. She actually laughed in my face!'

'Never liked her!'

'Yes, yes I know, me neither. She made my life hell for years. I don't know where I'd be now if I hadn't taken the time off for maternity leave and then the career break. If it wasn't for that, I'd say I'd be a broken woman, dealing with the wrath of the likes of Barbara, day in, day out.' I set the table for a light supper. A selection of mini bites from Marks and Spencers—vol au vents, sausage rolls and mini quiches.

'It's ready now, Declan. Come over.'

'Oh, I thought I smelled sausages.' He sounded eager. It wasn't long before his expression changed to one of disappointment though. As he got closer, he saw they weren't the fatty, fried, overly processed sausages he loved.

'Sausage rolls, Declan, or 'pork parcels', as I like to call them. You know, more sophisticated.

So, what about you? How are things in Give me a Brake?

'Oh yeah, mad busy, like yourself. Working late again.' He raised his eyes, exasperated, as he sat down.

'And how's Jim?' I enquired.

'Jim?'

'Yes, Jim. How is he?'

'Fine, fine I think. Y'know, I don't see him that much anymore. We're so busy in that place. No more than yourself, of course.'

'Mmmm, really? His wife, Claire, rang earlier. You left your wallet in the pub. Jim picked it up. She said he'll give it to you tomorrow.'

'Oh yeah, right, well, we did have a quick pint alright. Like I said, we're so overstretched, I hardly see him at work. That's why we caught up over a drink after.'

'Oh, I see. You weren't working late, then?'

'In fairness, I could have worked late tonight. We're fierce busy, that's no lie. Only, Jim fancied a beer and I ...' With that, he trailed off and we began eating our supper.

After a few minutes, Declan attempted to break the silence. 'The, eh, sausage rolls are tasty.'

'Pork parcels, Declan! They're pork parcels, remember?' I didn't mean to snap at him. It just came out that way.

After supper, I showed him his list of duties for

the morning. He glanced over it and then caught me by surprise as I was tidying up.

'So, you said that you asked Barbara if you could reduce your hours, didn't you? I don't remember you consulting me on that request. Isn't that the kind of thing we should talk about first?'

He touched a nerve. I could feel my brow furrowing. Ouch. He continued.

'And, if I remember correctly, you did the very same thing five years ago. You applied for a career break without letting me know. What plans have you got up your sleeve now? Anything I should know about?'

I carried on loading the dishwasher, until finally, I caved. 'It was a different time five and a half years ago when I applied for the career break. It was a new offer from my company, one which they had never offered before. If I didn't apply straight away, I would have missed out. There were so many others interested that I didn't think I'd get it, and that's why I didn't tell you. I thought there was no chance I'd get it.'

'Ok, I get that, but what about recently going behind my back? And asking to reduce your hours, while I'm working late almost every night of the week?'

'Declan, you have to understand, I miss spending my days with Lucy. I hate handing her over to someone else to mind. I'm her mother. I want to be the one taking her to school, walking her home and cooking her dinner. Nowadays, I barely make it home in time to put her to bed.'

'I know, Cara. I miss spending time with her too, but this is reality. All our friends are doing it—working full time, paying creche fees and just about managing to pay the mortgage. There's non-stop talk about childcare fees down in the club— they're all in the same predicament as us.'

'Ah, there you go again. The club, the club, the club...'

'There's decent, supportive people down there. Good friends of mine. You'd make some yourself if you ever came on down to support me and meet the other wives. They're always asking after you. They think they're not good enough for you anymore. Got notions, you have!'

I looked him straight in the eye, as I was on the verge of tears. He knew he had me now. In actual fact, I had tried to make friends and connect with the other women in the GAA, but I didn't fit in. I couldn't reach a common ground with them. I struggled to worm my way into their clique. They weren't nasty or anything, like the crowd at work, but it was obvious that we had nothing in common. They had no interest in the interior design magazines that I collected and I had no idea what team was playing who in the county final. I never knew the names of any players they gossiped about, so I gave up. I gave up trying.

When I look back now, it wasn't long after my mother had passed away, that I was meeting all of these new people. All at once too, still grieving my mother. Unfortunately, I was also feeling bullied and victimised at work through it all. I remember opening up to Declan at the time and he let me off the hook. He made excuses for why I couldn't attend the social nights out at the club.

Soon after, I became pregnant with Lucy, so I latched onto that for my non attendance vindication. No one expected anything of me, knowing how difficult it had been for us as a couple to conceive Lucy. No one asked anything of me and that suited me down to the ground. I could put all my energy into striving to recreate the mother/daughter bond I missed so acutely. She died only two years before Lucy was born.

'Cara, let's be realistic. We're both good at putting Lucy's best interests first, but we have to work as a team. We have to consult each other on major decisions like cutting our work hours. That affects the family finances. You see that, don't you?'

Damn it, he was right. I shouldn't have let that one slip. I should have consulted him, given I'd orchestrated the career break behind his back. Coupledom was still a learning curve for me. As Declan's friend, Jim, said, *'I'm my own woman'*.

Independent to the point of cutting my husband off. I'd get better at this, I would. One day.

I didn't quite have it in me to apologise, but I did humbly acknowledge through squinting eyes that he had a point. 'Yes, Declan, that sounds like a perfectly reasonable thing to do.' Then, I handed him a steaming mug of milky hot chocolate to tuck into. He seemed satisfied with that, so I excused myself and went upstairs to apply an anti-aging face mask. Uhhh, all that stress and furrowing …

Chapter Three

I HAD TO drag myself out of bed. Another damn sleepless night. I couldn't even blame Lucy's unsettled sleeping habits for this one. Work was constantly on my mind. I was, by nature, a most organised person, a planner, but the amount of work thrown my way was insurmountable. It was like they were punishing me for taking the five-year career break.

I was aware that due to renewing my time off, year on year, I'd prevented others from applying for a career break. There was only a limited number given each year. No one expected me to take more than one to two years, but I kept looking and finding loopholes in the system by reading the small print. In the end, I asserted my right to take the maximum of five years off. I seemed to be paying the price for it now though, at the hands of Barbara and her cronies. I was sure I was getting twice as much paperwork to do than the others, but every time I queried it, I was met with—

'Oh, times have changed since you left for your career break, Cara. The audits are more frequent and significantly more intense. Everyone has to pull their weight.'

Bullshit! I thought. I was definitely being given far more than my fair share of the workload. I knew it and they knew it! Yet, no one had a shred of sympathy for me. I had hoped the new moms in the office would give me the time of day, but all I got was—

'Sure you're grand, you only have one! I have three little ones at home.' Or—

'You've just had five years off! You can't complain!' Or—

'If you managed financially during your career break, why don't you just quit?'

They didn't know that I'd clocked up quite a bit of debt while on career break. We were still repaying the hard won IVF loan and our tracker had expired, so the mortgage had actually increased in recent years. Giving up work simply wasn't an option.

Just like at the GAA club, I felt ostracised by my work colleagues too. And I had no spare time to catch up with my own friends either, granted they were few and far between. I'd lost touch with so many acquaintances since the birth of Lucy. I suppose I intentionally made her the centre of my life at the expense of everything and everyone else.

I don't even know if I was aware of what I was doing. The current isolation I felt was compounded by sleep deprivation and I had this eerie feeling that something was gonna give.

'Cara, will you cover for me? I have to nip out to collect my daughter from playschool. Her granny usually does it, but she's sick today.'

'Oh, but I haven't had my break yet!' I replied.

'C'mon, Cara, I thought you of all people would understand. I can't just leave her at play-school, can I?'

'Em, no, I don't suppose you can. Off you go then.'

This meant I didn't finish up until after six that evening.

THE STRESS OF the daily grind continued. The start time got earlier. The finish time, later. The pressure was on Declan to be here, there and everywhere. It warmed his heart to share with me how Lucy skipped out of the minder's everyday as happy as Larry. He thought I'd be pleased to know how well she was getting on in Emma's 'House of Fun'.

I didn't say it, but it actually made me feel worse. It was like a dagger in my heart. My baby didn't need me anymore. She didn't miss me.

I couldn't finish my dinner that evening and

Declan commented. 'You look like you're losing weight, Cara. Are you looking after yourself?'

'You know, I think I only had a latte for my lunch today. It's chaotic in the office. We're desperately short-staffed. I reckon I'm carrying out the duties of five people.'

The next day in the office, I was hoping to leave by 5.30, when an impromptu call came in, together with a dozen folders thrown on my desk at the last minute. Of course, everything had to be done immediately, thoroughly and by the book, which I'd always been a firm believer in, but now that my circumstances had changed and I was a mother, I would have greatly appreciated some leeway. I got up to fill my coffee cup. No wonder my sleep routine is messed up, I thought, as I gulped it down. I got regular bouts of caffeine jitters, but noticed many others in the office seemed to suffer the same affliction, with twitching eyelids and shaking hands.

Kate gave me a fright, as she hollered over my shoulder. 'Cara, there are interviews this Saturday morning. Barbara wants you to be on the interview panel since you're one of the senior members of staff. Be here at 10am. Should be finished up by two, I'd say.'

'On Saturday? I can't work on a Saturday! That's my family time!'

'She just said to tell you to be here. She never

mentioned there was a choice... Sorry!'

'But I, I can't...'

There was no point. The messenger had disappeared already. No one had time to wait around for responses anymore. Once the necessary information was divulged, people just moved on.

This place is taking over my life, I sobbed to myself. Tears streamed from my eyes as I quietly returned to my desk, with my head hung low. I sat there staring into space for a little while and blatantly ignored the incoming call. It kept ringing, so I unplugged the phone. I looked down at the sheets of paper on my desk. They were smudged with black tearstains. I briefly contemplated giving up wearing mascara, before picking up my mobile to call the childminder.

'Hi Emma, can you put Lucy on please?'

'Cara, is everything okay?'

'Yes, I just want to talk to Lucy.'

I overheard the exchange. The refusal, followed by the command and the final response. I didn't think my heart could sink any lower, but it did. Emma came back on the line.

'Sorry, Cara, she's painting and doesn't want to talk. She said she'd see you at bedtime tonight ... if you're home. Is that okay or do you want me to try again?'

'No, Emma,' I gasped, trying hard to rein it in. 'No thanks, I can hear she's busy. She sounds happy. She's always happy in your care.'

'She is, Cara, she really is. There's no need to worry about her, okay?'

'I know. You do a fantastic job caring for her and I … I just want to say thanks. I really appreciate it.'

Then, I hung up. I didn't want Emma to hear me weeping. The truth was I thought she was too good at her job. So efficient that Lucy didn't miss me. She was getting too independent now. I wasn't ready for this. She's only five years old for Christ's sake. I thought about calling Declan, but realised he'd probably just tell me to pull myself together and that wouldn't help at all. Who else could I call now, in my hour of need?

I was aware that some of my co-workers were glancing my way. They either heard my sobs or saw my black tears. Not one of them came over to ask if I was okay. I looked down and realised my hands were shaking. My breathing quickened and I suddenly started to panic. What was happening to me? My stomach clenched and I retched, but nothing came out. I knew I had to get out of the office.

On my way out the door, I was met with a delivery of ten CVs to read through for the interviews and check all references before the next morning. Homework, as well as working way over and above the amount of hours I was being paid for! And being asked to come in at the weekend! That was the last straw! How dare they!

In moments of deep distress, I had this habit of dropping to my knees. It was as if the folder of CVs were a sack of potatoes and I just fell there and then. My body gave way and I transitioned to horizontal. Lipstick rolled from my handbag, keys slid across the floor and CVs scattered everywhere.

There was a stunned silence. All eyes were on me. I could feel it. No one seemed to know what to say or do. I just lay there. I didn't want anyone to come over, preferring to be left alone and oddly not caring so much that I was sprawled out on the floor. I fell into some sort of trance, or did I faint? Whatever it was, it felt wonderful. I seemed light-headed, as if a burden had been lifted. I sensed the lines in my forehead falling apart, giving up their rigidity in acknowledgement that they didn't need to be there. I felt my breath deepening and slowing down and realised my hands weren't shaking any longer. I just lay there and stared into oblivion.

My peaceful bliss was interrupted when Kate anxiously approached and reached out her hand, whispering. 'Are you okay, Cara?' I didn't respond, but I looked her in the eye and smiled. She looked around uncomfortably, willing somebody to come over. Others shuffled over and began making efforts to help me up. They sat me on a chair and forced me to drink some water. I could hear them ringing Declan to come and get me, but I remained motionless throughout. This was so unlike me, but I felt at peace. Broken, but at peace.

The company doctor had already left the building and I overheard conversations about whether or not they should call an ambulance. Kate mentioned that Declan was on his way, but Barbara was thinking along the lines of saving the company from a possible case of medical negligence if they failed to call a doctor. That was just the way her mind worked. I continued to smile to myself, feeling surprisingly chilled out.

When Declan arrived, they filled him in and he reassured them he would handle it from here, saying not to call an ambulance. If he thought I needed medical attention, he would attend to it later. He just wanted to get me home for now. Kate gathered up my things from the floor and together, Declan and Barbara held me up and walked me out to the car. My legs felt like jelly and I wasn't much help to them. Declan carried most of my weight. I lay my head back in the passenger seat and closed my eyes. I was thoroughly exhausted after all that.

When we arrived home, Declan's mother, Cathy, greeted us. She had gotten a taxi over to mind Lucy and put her to bed. When she saw me, she put her hand over her mouth in shock. Declan sat me down on the couch and I overheard Cathy's concern about my pale, vacant expression. That's exactly how I felt. Vacant. I had no worry left in me. The stress of work lifted. They saw me at my lowest this evening. I always cared so much what they thought of me, but in my fragile, post melt-down state, I felt serene. I felt like a winner.

And then a few minutes later, I began to feel incredibly tired again, like I was in the car, so I laid my head back on the couch. I couldn't fall asleep though, because I started to get flashbacks of the faces of my colleagues as they examined me on the floor. Oh no, their expressions weren't sympathet-ic. They were clearly horrified at the grotesque scene before them. Their esteemed colleague spread out on the floor, legs splayed, mouth hanging open in a demonic smile, probably drooling. Yes, I think I remember the drool running down my cheek. Oh God, I started to panic. I let out a roar and my body shook. Declan pegged it over to me. He shook me.

'Cara, Cara, are you okay? Calm down, Cara. You're home now.'

'What's happening to her, Declan?' Cathy shouted.

'I don't know. I think she's having a panic at-tack. What'll I do, Mam?'

Cathy reached for her handbag. 'Here, give her this. It's a sleeping pill. My doctor prescribes them to me, but I use them sparingly. I've got loads of extra ones.'

Declan got a glass of water, while I almost passed out on the couch. I was sweating too, or was I drooling again? I'm not sure which bodily fluid it was, but it ran down my face and dripped down my neck.

'Actually, Declan, they're quite strong. Just give her a half,' Cathy warned. Declan did as he was told and uttered something else. Then, he picked me up in his strong arms that I hardly ever gave him credit for, and put me to bed.

The last thing I heard him say to Cathy was, 'She's too good at her job, Mam. They're taking advantage of her.'

✧ ✧ ✧

THE NEXT MORNING I awoke with a start. 'Where am I?' I blurted out as if I was still mid-dream. But no one answered me. There was no one there. I spotted the note on the bedside locker.

I'm at work. Lucy's at school and Emma's picking her up. I'll collect her after work. I rang your office and told them you wouldn't be in for a few days. You better get a cert from the doctor. Ring me if you need anything.

x Declan

I lay there and tried to piece together the events of the previous day. Let's see, I remembered falling in the office, the alarmed expressions of my co-workers and the overwhelming sense I'd experienced at the time, of simply not caring. Yes, I didn't give a hoot about what those backstabbers thought of me!

A smile swept over my face. *What's happening to me? Why do I feel no shame? Is this the dawn of a midlife crisis? If so, it feels pretty good so far.* I was beginning to understand the buzz Walter White must have felt when he began to break bad. *Could this be the female version of his metamorphosis? Is this the beginning of the end for me?* I pondered this potential change of direction in my life, as I wrapped myself in my Ted Baker clove print dressing gown with matching slippers.

I also fondly remembered Declan coming to my rescue, and the only other outstanding memory was that pill I got from Cathy. It was like a miracle cure! What was it Declan asked his mother right before he placed it in my mouth and instructed me to wash it down with some water? Oh yes, he asked, 'Mam, are you sure it's okay to give this to her?'

And Cathy's reply. 'Ah Declan, look at the poor creature. She's having a nervous breakdown. She needs rest. Of course it's perfectly reasonable to give her a little something to help her sleep.'

Chapter Four

I HAULED MYSELF up in disbelief that I'd just slept for thirteen hours straight! I showered, got dressed and made coffee, all the while that devilish grin still lingering on my face. I Googled the local GP surgery on MacMillan Road. I rang to check if they could fit me in.

'Hi, I need an appointment as soon as possible, please.'

'Name, please?'

'Cara Cawley,' I replied.

'38 Cedarwood Drive?'

'Yes, that's me.'

'28th of the 3rd, nineteen seventy s....'

'Yes, yes. I'm still in my thirties. Can you note that, please?'

'Mrs Cawley, you last attended Dr Khan. I can give you an appointment with him tomorrow morning at 11.30am. Is that okay?'

'No. Anything today? It's an emergency.'

'Oh, yes of course. Dr Dempsey at 1.45pm?'

'Right, right, I'll take it.'

'And how will you be paying us today, Mrs Cawley?'

'What? I haven't even had my appointment yet and you're asking for payment? I could be on my deathbed, about to be told I have weeks, even days to live, and you're …'

'Excuse me, Mrs Cawley, we like to confirm payment in advance. Cash or card?'

The cheek, the nerve, I mean …

'Mrs Cawley? Do you still want the appointment this afternoon? Is payment a problem for you?

'No. I'll be there. Credit card.' Oh, maybe that sounded a bit shouty. There was silence on the line. Then, the receptionist spoke very quietly, almost a whisper.

'Thank you, Mrs Cawley. Could you call out your credit card number please?'

'Uhhhhhh.' She must have either heard my loud sigh or my heart rate quicken.

'I hope I haven't caused you distress with this request for payment?' she offered.

Oh, you duplicitous piece of … 'What? No. Me? No, it's a perfectly reasonable request,' I assured her before rattling off my card number.

❖   ❖   ❖

MY CAR WASN'T in the driveway. Oh yes, it was

still in the office car park, as Declan had collected me in his van. I was left with no alternative but to get the bus. I honestly couldn't remember the last time I'd done something so pedestrian as getting the bus. I found it presented an ideal opportunity to people-watch, intently. Now, as a rule, I'm not one to pass comments, but as I observed the other passengers from a safe distance, I noticed greasy hair, dirty fingernails and noisy, obnoxious teenagers. Those brats should be in school, I mused.

When I arrived in Dr Seán Dempsey's fresh-smelling, modern, purpose-built waiting room, I flicked through some fashion magazines. I tried not to make eye contact with other waiting patients for fear I'd catch their diseases. I kept my head stuck in the magazine and realised most of the clothes on the models would look great on me. I had the figure to pull them off. In fact, why was I always wearing the same thing? I was so unadventurous in my clothing. Why was that? That was something I could and should change during my forthcoming days off work on sick leave. Oh yes, I intended to milk this. There was no way I would go back to that hell hole of an office for at least two weeks. I made plans in my head of what I might get up to...

1. Catch up with Margot and Beatrice (my besties, whom I'd hardly seen since Lucy was born)

2. Go shopping and replace my whole, boring wardrobe
3. Get more of those magic pills, so I'd bloody well sleep through the night from now on
4. Take Lucy to the playground, playzone, circus, cinema and panto
5. Go to a spa
6. Visit the beautician and hairdresser to address lines and length in that order
7. Take that online assertiveness course that I'd so often threatened to do
8. Get more of those pills

'Cara Cawley?' At last! I beamed, dropping the magazine back with such a clatter that it frightened me and seemingly some of the elderly waiting patients too. I noticed them jump with alarm. *Whoops!*

The doctor's office was clinical but smelled of aromatic aftershave. The young doctor caught my eye immediately, as he marched over to introduce himself and shake my hand. 'Seán Dempsey. Pleased to meet you.' I found myself going quite giddy and accidentally let out a high-pitched giggle. I was overcome by the doctor's piercing blue eyes, his firm handshake and his youth. He looked as if he was barely twenty.

'What … what age are you?' I blurted out mid-giggle.

'Oh!' He seemed taken aback. 'I'm thirty-one.'

'You, you look a lot younger!' I smiled wide-eyed and blinking, or were my eyelids fluttering, perhaps?

'So, what brings you here, Mrs Cawley?'

'Call me Cara, please! I, I, well, em, you see, it's a little hard to explain. I, I em ...'

'Take your time.'

Oh my God, this man is simply beautiful. He's so ... distracting.

'Yes, well, I think I had a nervous breakdown at work yesterday. You see, I haven't been sleeping lately, at all actually, and I'm struggling to cope with my workload in the office. In fact, I think I'm being bullied and victimised at work by my boss and one or two colleagues. And I'm finding it hard to devote time to my daughter, as I'm so stressed with work and so sleep deprived. And I miss our relationship from when I was a stay-at-home mom. We did everything together and now I can barely make time for her on the weekends, between catching up on housework and shopping and visiting family and ...'

I seemed to just trail off. I had no words left and I was so darn tired. I stared into space, in sorrow, as pre-career break flashbacks of victimisation in the workplace came to mind. Like when Kate accidentally forgot to inform me about the birthday fund. My colleagues thought I was too stingy to contribute, yet I'd show up for free cocktails. I didn't know Kate collected money for it each month and when I eventually found out, she thought it would look good and save my reputation if I donated a back payment, even charging me for the celebratory nights that I didn't attend.

And of course, there was Barbara, with her cutting remarks and sarcastic jokes about me being straightlaced and fussy. I knew she called me the 'RBF' behind my back, alluding to my Resting Bitch Face. With my furrowed brow and tense expression, I couldn't manifest an alternative resting face. My muscles naturally relaxed into such a facial gesture. There was nothing I could do about it. On one occasion, she told me that was probably why I couldn't find a man. The others in the office were all coupled up long before I met Declan.

'And? Cara, please go on.'

'Hmmm? Oh, okay.'

'Yes?' He raised his shapely, fair eyebrows that seemed to hold the exact amount of fur on them that eyebrows should have. No more or no less. Perfect eyebrows.

'I hate my boss and all of my work colleagues. I hate them.'

'Okay, is that it?'

'No, I hate all of my husband's friends, which also happen to be our closest family friends, because I don't see my own friends anymore.'

'Mmm hmmm.' He was vigorously scribbling notes.

'And…'

'Yes, Cara?' He met my eye.

'And I, I hate my …' I got momentarily distracted by his look of concern. Distracted in a mesmerising kind of way. 'Oh, you have, you have very … You have … eyes.' It was as if he cast a spell upon me.

We held eye contact. The blue of his, piercing the grey of mine. There was a long pause, before the doctor spoke again.

'Right, you've got quite a bit going on there, Cara. There seems to be a lot of stress in your life and a fair bit of conflict too. You've certainly got relationship issues that need addressing.'

'Thank you, Doctor.'

'Hmmm? For what?'

'For listening. I've somehow managed to be more honest with you in the past five minutes than I've been with anyone in my whole life! I mean, I've never even been that honest with myself before!'

'Sometimes when we reach a crisis point and have a breakdown, as you mentioned, our inner pain bubbles to the surface. It's like all those issues that you bottled up for years just explode out of you all of a sudden. Your system is at breaking point.'

'Oh yes, Doctor, it is. I was hoping you could help me?'

'Well, let's see. I'd like you to get your bloods done and check your hormone levels and I can certainly help you with your stress-related illness.'

I couldn't help smiling. *He thinks I have an illness!*

'And I can offer a temporary measure to get you back on track with your sleeping pattern. As for your other issues, the em...the "hate" issues, I'd like to recommend a very reputable counsellor to you. Have you ever tried therapy before, Cara?'

'Why Docta, no. No, I haven't. I'll think about that tomorrow. After all, tomorrow is ...' *Hmmm ... Why am I suddenly sounding like Scarlett O'Hara?*

'Okay, Cara, that's fine. Would you be prepared to go? I can write a referral note right here, right now?'

'Yes, yes of course. Whatever you recommend, Doctor. I'll try it. I mean, I'll try anything and I mean ANYTHING!' I stared wide-eyed into Doctor Seán's eyes and noticed him shifting uncomfortably in his chair. Once again, I relished in the feeling that I had him right where I wanted him. In the palm of my hand.

After swallowing a gulp of air, Seán replied.

'Please, Cara, call me Seán. That's great that

you're prepared to give therapy a go. Not everyone is so willing. You know, some people are very private, like a closed book.'

'Oh, no, not me, Doc, I mean, Seán. I'm wide open.' Ooooh. This time it was my turn to take a gulp and wipe the sweat from my brow.

I clarified, 'I mean, I used to be introverted and ... bu ... but now I realise that hasn't worked for me. It's time now, time for me to reach out and share my problems. Yes, I think therapy would be a godsend to me at this moment in time.'

'Yes, I agree. It's good to talk. I'll do that referral letter for you now. And I'm prescribing a low dose of benzodiazepine, to help with your stress levels when you return to work. We don't want you having another breakdown. It should also help settle your head at night and grant you a sound night's sleep.'

'Yes, about that, Doc, I mean, Seán. My mother-in-law gave me half, only a half of a sleeping pill last night and to tell you the truth, it worked wonders for me. I just thought that you could possibly prescribe me a supply, and I'd only use them when I'm having real trouble sleeping. Just a half at a time. What d'you think?'

'Well, as I said, Cara, the benzodiazepine will relax you and help reduce your stress levels and this will have a knock-on effect on your sleep.'

'So you say, Seán, and I'm sure you're right

about that. But you see, I've never in my life had such a complete night's sleep as I did last night. I mean yesterday I hit rock bottom, ROCK BOTTOM! And today ... Well, I'm on top of the world! And I really believe that tiny pill I took last night, just a half as I said, but I think that miniscule dot may just have saved my life! I mean, if I didn't take that and get a sound night's sleep last night, then who knows what I might have done?'

'What do you mean?'

I contorted my face by raising one eyebrow higher than the other and dropping one side of my mouth. I'm sure my brow furrowed repugnantly. I was glad there were no mirrors in sight, so I didn't have to behold my own reflection. I was aiming to incite terror and judging by Seán's reaction, I succeeded.

Seán queried, 'Did you have dark thoughts, Cara? Is that what you're trying to tell me?'

'If I said yes, then would you think about giving me those tiny, little pills, Doctor, I mean, Seán?'

'Well, if you think it would restore a sense of calm to your life and prevent you feeling those depressive thoughts on the grounds of sleep deprivation, then, yes, I could prescribe you with a week's supply and we'll see how you go. I think that's perfectly reasonable, Cara.'

Chapter Five

Barefoot, naked, except for a crown of olive leaves draped around my head, I padded through the woods. My long, dark hair brushed my bare shoulders, tickling my neck and chest. I was looking, yearning, searching for someone, but who? I felt raw, wild and free in my nakedness. I sank in mud, stepped on thorns, swung from branches to find what I was looking for. I didn't care who saw me and I wasn't scared of the animals hiding behind the trees. I was alive, weightless and unburdened. This was what living should be, I told myself. Boom! There it was! The thing that I'd been searching for. I stood at the edge of a large, grassy hole in the forest ground. I looked down and felt my heart leap. I closed my eyes and fell forward, down, down, down, until I landed on a bed of feathers. He was there, waiting for me with pills in his hands. I reached for him shouting, 'Doctor Seán!'

'Christ above, Cara, will you wake up! I can't listen to this anymore! It's been a whole week of you screaming out crying or howling like a wolf in your sleep. I can't tell what you're doing or saying anymore, but it's doing my head in! You better get yourself back to that doctor and tell him those pills are giving you nightmares and making you go batty!' Declan was livid. Apparently, I'd been keeping him awake all week.

I could feel my brow furrowing in confusion. Oh, that was just a dream. Damn, I thought, but then I scrunched up my eyes excitedly in response to Declan's request.

'Yes, oh yes, I must go back to Doctor Seán. You're right! I must go to him!'

Declan rolled over to get out of bed.

'I suppose I'll get Lucy up and ready for school again.'

'Thanks, Declan.'

'When, eh, when d'you think you might be back on your feet again? It's just that I missed all the training sessions during the week, but I was still hoping to play a match tomorrow.'

'Oh, yes, well, I'll go back to the doctor today and see what he thinks of me.' Internal swoon. 'But I think it's best if you drop Lucy to your mother's tomorrow. Em, maybe for a sleepover ... for the weekend? Wouldn't she love that?'

'Well, eh, yeah, I suppose they both would. But

what do you think you'll be doing? Are you over the nervous breakdown yet?'

'No, no I'm not. I'm at the tail end of it though, so don't be worried.'

'Oh, oh right. Is that how it works? So, how long more do you expect…?'

'I'll just go and see what the doctor says, alright?'

'Yeah, yeah, good luck with that. Tell him those pills are making you howl through the night though, won't you?'

As soon as Declan left, I sank back in the sheets and closed my eyes. It was so easy to drift off with those sleeping pills still in my system. So easy to get back into the …

Where am I? I looked down. Naked again? I must be dreaming. 'I know you're here', I shouted. There was no response, but I could make out the shape of a figure behind the clouds. Broad shoulders, an athletic build and a mop of blonde hair came towards me. 'I know it's you, Doctor. I know it's you.' I reached out towards the figure and he swept me up into his arms. 'Where are you taking me?' I asked, staring lovingly into his eyes. 'We will bathe together in the river, my love', he declared. I beamed and melted, as was my usual response to his commands. 'The water will wash away the venom on your scales', he said. 'Wait, my what? What are you talking about?'

The alarm I felt must have knocked me out of my dream. I jumped out of bed immediately. *I need more of those pills!*

A half an hour later, I strutted into the waiting room, not a care in the world. You better be ready for me, Doctor Seán! I'm coming for you! I roared with my private, internal voice. I loved that voice. I could get away with anything with that voice. I sat down and sifted through the same fashion magazines, but this time, noted the brands and shops of my favourite items of clothing. Mostly the lingerie collections caught my eye. I inhaled deeply and considered the fact that I needed to upgrade everything in my life, from the inside ... out.

'Cara Cawley?'

I instantly felt a surge of femininity rise within me. I'd never experienced these heights before, yet could identify what it was straight away. I barged into Doctor Seán's surgery, announcing, 'I'm here, Seán, I'm here!'

'Oh, Mrs Cawley, hello! Please take a seat.'

'It's Cara, remember? First name terms. And you're Seán.'

'Indeed! Cara, how has your week been? How are you feeling?'

Slow, sensual intake of breath, 'Oh wonderful, Seán, I just feel wonderful!'

'Excellent! So the meds have helped reduce your stress levels, I take it?'

'Hmmm?'

'And you've been getting good sleep at night, I trust? You look very well rested.'

'Huh?'

'Did you get a chance to ring the therapist yet? If there's a waiting list, I could suggest an alternative one.'

'A wha…? Oh, oh em, well just there when I said I was feeling wonderful, that was … em, that was just a fff … fleeting feeling. What I meant was, I don't feel wonderful, quite the opposite in fact. Dreadful! I meant to say I was feeling dreadful, Seán. Just dreadful!'

'Oh? I actually thought you seemed a lot perkier than last week?'

'Haha, perkier!' I laughed, but promptly turned serious. 'I mean, no, it may seem that way, but no, unfortunately it's just a facade.'

'Why do you feel the need to pretend, Cara? You said last week that it felt good to be honest with everyone, including yourself.'

'I think that was the high I experienced, post breakdown.'

'I've never heard of that!'

'Yes, and now that I've come down, I feel reality creeping back and the prospect of going back to work is looming. I actually feel every muscle in my body and mind tensing up on account of this. In fact, I think if I returned to work now, I'd go straight downhill again. I'm on seriously shaky ground, Doctor, eh, I mean, Seán.'

'Oh, I'm sorry you feel like that. I suppose it's early days in your recovery. I mean it was just about a week ago that you had your episode. You need to address your issues, Cara, before you go back to work. I'll extend your cert for a month and this gives you time to get a few therapy sessions in and hopefully, you'll be up and running with that by the time you go back to work. Don't expect a miracle cure, but you'll have a crutch to get you through the low times.'

'A month? Thank you, that affords me some time to get better. The meds are certainly improving my stress levels, but what I really feel is important to me at this point in my recovery is getting a good night's sleep. Those sleeping pills, they actually seem to...'

'You may not be experiencing the same volume of stress now that you're off work, Cara. I could probably reduce the benzodiazepine dosage for the moment. I can always increase it, if needs be, when you go back to work. And if you think the pills are helping, how about I prescribe enough for a month?'

I let out an excited squeal, 'Ahhhh!'

Seán looked up. 'Hmmm?'

'Oh nothing! Thank you, Seán. Just knowing that I have those to use if I need them calms me down tremendously!'

'Your bloods have come back normal, so that's good news! Now, would you like me to make that therapy appointment for you, Cara?'

'Oh no, you've got enough to do. I'll do that, Seán. You've a full waiting room of patients out there to see. You mind yourself now and ... thank you,' I beamed, amid the uncontrollable flutter of my eyelids.

✧　✧　✧

I STOPPED IN Risqué Lingerie on my way home to stock up on some of that new season lingerie I'd seen in the magazine. I also picked up my prescription at the chemist, kissing the little box of sleeping pills when I received them, much to the pharmacist's surprise! Then, I browsed around clothes shops, looking at bright coloured fabrics and tight, above-the-knee skirts. I caressed silky blouses and imagined Seán's fingers dancing over the top buttons before undoing ...

'Ah, Cara! How are you?'

'Oh, hi ... B...Bernadette! How are you?' I answered, snapping out of my daze. *Grrr, how dare she ...*

'I'm grand! I met Declan yesterday. He said you

were out sick from work?'

'Yeah, I'm feeling a bit better now.'

'Ah good, you'll be back to work on Monday then, will you?'

'Actually, no, Bernadette. I just got a cert for a month. You know, to rest and recover ...'

'Oh I see, sure won't Lucy be delighted to have Mammy at home again!'

Suddenly, I had a lightbulb moment! I couldn't wait to get home and share my wonderful idea with Declan. Later that evening, when Lucy went to bed, I discussed it with him on the chesterfield over tea and cakes.

He didn't respond quite as I hoped. 'You what? You can't just go and take her out of the minder's for a month! She'll lose her place! There's a waiting list to get into Emma's. If she loses her place, what'll we do when you go back to work?'

'Don't think about that now. I have one month off. I don't want to consider work. I need to distance myself from it to aid my recovery.'

'Have you lost your marbles, Cara? It'll upset Lucy's routine to withdraw her from Emma's now. And I'm not paying her fees for a whole month if she's not gonna be there!'

'Declan, I'm her mother and I know best. If you don't want to pay to hold her place, then I'll find someone else to take her on. I want her here with me, like old times. Sure, the doctor might even extend my cert when he sees how well I'm getting on!'

'Are you off your rocker? Doctors give certs to people who are sick, not to people who are "getting on well"!'

I shifted sideways on the couch to reach his eye and show him how serious I was. 'Declan,' I began, 'I was at an all time low. You know that, you saw me. Look at me now, building myself up again. You should be proud of me, not making fun!'

'Did the doctor give you more pills?'

'Yes.'

'And do you have to take them for the whole month?'

'I do!' I could barely contain my excitement.

'Hmmm. And what does he want you to do on your month off?'

'Go to counselling or some sort of therapy.'

'Really?'

I sat back again on the couch. I didn't think we needed to maintain eye contact any longer. 'Look, they advise all their patients to do a bit of that. They have to these days, you know, to cover themselves and all that.'

'And are you going to do it?'

'Of course not. I don't need it!'

'Oh. But don't you think you should follow the doctor's advice?'

'No, well, he doesn't know. He doesn't need to know. At least, I'm not not going to tell him. It's my business anyway. I think that's perfectly reasonable, don't you?'

Chapter Six

I ENGAGED IN some online shopping over the next few days. I supposed it would look bad to be seen out and about in the shops when I was on sick leave. I was still receiving full pay, so that alleviated some of the guilt I felt when purchasing what one could only describe as non-essential goods, such as a glass magazine display stand and a range of *Home and Living* magazines to put in it. There was too much choice out there. I literally felt under pressure when trying to choose which ones would look best on display. Just when I clicked my final purchase for the day, I heard the front door. Lucy must have heard it too. 'Daddy!' she roared and I imagined he swung her around a few times. She'd insist he did and Declan found it hard to refuse her. He left her in the playroom and burst into the kitchen with a big bunch of flowers.

'You didn't need to do that, Declan. I thought we were saving our money. They look like they cost a fortune.'

'Cara, you're out sick from work! I thought

they might cheer you up?'

'Being out sick from work is enough to cheer me up!' I noticed his face fell a little, so I thanked him with a peck on the cheek and put them on the counter. I checked on Lucy in the playroom, where I'd set up a painting station for her. She looked at me with weary eyes. 'Mommy, I think that's enough painting for me today. Can I watch cartoons now?' I hung her paintings to dry. So talented she was, and only five years old. She reminded me of me as a little girl. There was nothing I couldn't put my hand to. I switched on the TV and returned to the kitchen, where Declan was putting the flowers into a vase. He turned when he heard me.

'You do know you have to return to work at some point, don't you? We're in a lot of debt, y'know. It was always the plan to repay those loans as soon as you were earning again.'

'Yes, yes, yes, but I don't want to think about that now. Let me enjoy this precious time off with Lucy, right?'

'I was thinking about what the doctor said. Y'know, about the counselling? Well ... maybe we should go together, like, to marriage counselling. Some of the lads in the club have done it and resolved issues with their other halves. We've been through a lot, Cara. Those years of IVF took their toll on our marriage. And then when Lucy was born, you sort of shut me out of the family in a way.'

'No, no, Declan, that's not true. You wanted nothing more than to go back training and playing matches. Don't you remember?'

'I remember I wanted nothing more than to enjoy my new family, spend quality time at home with my two girls and take you out to the park and the zoo and the pet farm. But you vetoed all my suggestions. You always had better or more important things to do with Lucy. It was like you got what you wanted from me, a baby, and you didn't need me anymore.'

'Declan! You've never said any of this before! What's gotten into you?'

'It was just when you mentioned going for counselling. I thought, well, I thought it might be something we could do together.'

'No, no, not in my current condition.'

'Y'know, when I think back now, it's lucky I had the club to turn to back then. All the lads, they were a great support to me and ...'

That's when I yawned. 'Yeah, that's great, De-clan, the club and that ... Do you know what? I think I'll grab one of those pills now and have an early night. You don't mind, do you? You'll put Lucy to bed, won't you?'

'Oh, I thought we were having a serious con-versation about our marriage and ...'

'I'm still in recovery after the nervous break-down. Can we talk about this some other time? I think it's perfectly reasonable for me to have an early night every now and then, don't you?'

✧   ✧   ✧

I followed the footprints in the snow. The size of the footprints and the shape in-formed me my muse had perfectly formed feet. Of course, I knew exactly who they belonged to. Now if only I could find him... 'Seán, Seán, I need you, I need more pills. I'm running out. I've only two left. Where are you, Seán?' *I felt a shiver and my feet were becoming numb in the snow. I looked down. Naked! Again! Why? Always bloody naked, even in these Baltic conditions.* 'Seán, where are you? I'll catch my death out here. Come out, I need you. Please!' *Suddenly, a figure appeared in the distance, draped in animal skin and fur.* 'Seán, is that you?' *I howled, wrapping my arms around my now violently shivering body. The figure approached, carrying something. It looked like the carcass of a dead animal. My body was turning blue and I fell to my knees. Pangs of chilblain shot up through my knees.* 'Save me, Seán, save me!'

I screamed over and over again until I woke myself up. I was still panting, traumatised, and in a sweat. I spotted a note on the bedside locker.

You were having very stressful dreams. You kept waking me up, so I slept in the spare room. Go to the doctor and change your medication. Those pills don't agree with you!

X Declan

I thought about the pills and realised I wouldn't be able to function after a restless night like last night. Usually, I actually enjoyed the erotic dreams that the pills gifted me, but last night's was both stressful and disturbing. I didn't feel well rested at all, but rather exhausted and drained. I wanted to go back to sleep.

A few hours later, Declan arrived home on his lunch break and woke me up.

'Cara, are you still asleep? No one could get a hold of you! The doctor rang, wondering why you didn't show up for your appointment. He said you weren't answering your phone. What's wrong with you, Cara?'

'Oh, oh no, I must have fallen back to sleep. What time is it?'

'It's half past one. Look, you go and have a shower. I'll collect Lucy. Ring the doctor, okay? He sounded concerned.'

'Really? Seán was concerned about me?'

'Yes, especially when I told him those pills are making you more tired. They're doing the exact opposite of what they're meant to do.'

'Ah Declan, the pills are working fine. Seán was asking for me? Was he?'

'Doctor Seán, your doctor, Cara. And em, the receptionist rang too.'

I raised my eyes. 'What did she have to say?'

'She had to charge your credit card, because you never cancelled your appointment. There was a €60 fee for a no-show.'

He looked as if he expected me to feel guilty, but I felt nothing. Even hearing that Seán was asking for me didn't lift my mood. I turned my head to the side and Declan gave up.

'Cara, ring and make another appointment, okay!' He went downstairs.

I hauled myself out of bed and into the shower. Ooooh, my body felt like stone. I had to drag it along behind me. I'd never felt heavier. The water from the shower hurt me. I couldn't stay in for too long. I got out and wrapped myself in a towel and started crying. Unstoppable tears ran down my cheeks. I felt nothing but hopelessness.

When Declan returned, he found me sobbing on the floor in the bathroom. He didn't seem to know what to say and I was in a heap. I suppose he'd never seen me like this and I think he got a fright.

'Wait here, pet. Wait here, I'll be back.'

He went and dropped Lucy in with our next door neighbour, Bernadette. I was shivering by the time he got back. Not a word was exchanged. He picked me up, dried me off and helped me put on my Ted Baker clove print dressing gown. He held me steady as we walked downstairs and he made me some tea and toast.

'Don't you have to get back to work?' I asked.

'I rang in and told them you weren't well.'

'Is Lucy in Emma's, yeah?'

'Cara, Lucy's place is gone in the childminder's. Emma had a waiting list, so someone has taken Lucy's spot. We'll have to go on the waiting list as soon as you're ready to go back to w....'

'Oh, oh yeah I forgot. We can't send her to Emma's anymore.'

'She's next door with Bernadette. They're bringing Rex to the park. I said to send her in when they get back. Bernadette was only delighted to have her. She's lonely now, since Roger passed away.'

'Yeah, yeah she is.'

'I tried ringing the doctor back, but they're closed for today. I think your best bet is to go into the clinic first thing in the morning and wait until he can see you. You might be there half the day, but if you ring in tomorrow looking for an appointment, you probably won't get one until next week, with it being a Friday.'

'Yeah, I really need to get another cert, don't I?'

'Well, you don't seem ready to go back to work any time soon. See what he says.'

I looked up at Declan and we locked eyes. 'Thanks Declan, thanks for everything.' He smiled back with his kind, innocent blue eyes, full of compassion.

✧   ✧   ✧

THE NEXT MORNING, Declan dropped Lucy to school and me to the doctor's. I didn't feel well enough to drive there alone. The receptionist looked as if she felt bad for charging me yesterday. She promised to fit me in. I didn't have to wait too long in the end.

'Cara, come in! I expected to see you yesterday. How have you been?'

'Oh yeah, I'm sorry about that. I … I…' Oh, I didn't know what to say.

'You seem … tired, Cara. Have you been sleeping?'

'No, well yes, but not proper sleep. I've been dreaming a lot, kind of hallucinating, I think. I … I used to like it, the dreams or hallucinations or whatever you want to call them, but lately I don't like them so much. I don't like what's happening and I especially don't like how I feel when I wake up afterwards.'

'Yes, your husband told me you've been having restless nights. How have you been feeling during the day? Have you been groggy or listless?'

'I seemed to have energy the first week or so, but lately, yes, I've been feeling lethargic and lazy. I keep wanting to go back to bed. I've never been like this.'

'Your husband also mentioned your reluctance to speak to a therapist.'

'Did he?' Hmmm, Declan hadn't told me about that.

'Yes, I'd still like you to talk to someone.'

'Okay, if you really want me to.'

'And I think you should try an antidepressant. You don't seem stressed and tense anymore, but I sense that you're feeling low and your husband seems concerned. Am I right?'

'I just feel sad. I want to cry all the time.' My head lowered into my hands.

'Talking to someone would help, I promise.'

'Can't I just keep coming to you and talking to you? I like talking to you and I feel comfortable here.'

'I'm a GP, Cara, not a psychologist. You can come to me initially, if you're more comfortable, though I will refer you to someone else in the long term. I'm going to try you on an antidepressant and different sleeping pills, not as strong. Will you come back next week to check in?'

'And what about work?'

'Don't worry, I'll give you another cert.'

Bingo! My stress levels lowered on the spot. I could feel my body softening. Every muscle unclenched simultaneously and I allowed myself to breathe. It felt good. The idea of another month off work lifted my spirits. I managed a respectful nod to Doctor Seán on my way out.

I had a few hours to kill in town before Lucy's collection from school. First, I got my meds in the chemist and checked out the cool looking shop next door. It was called Word Haven and it sold a selection of music and books. I was drawn to the self-help section straight away and stunned by the amount of books that screamed at me from the shelves, just from their titles alone. *Inner Peace*, *Be The Person You've Always Wanted To Be*, *How To Fall In Love With Your Husband* and my favourite, *Unleash The Beast Within*. They were quite pricey, so I just picked up the last title. For starters, I told myself, knowing full well that I wanted to read every single one of them from cover to cover, as soon as I could afford them.

I was delighted with my choice and began devouring it on the bus journey home. This is going to change my life, I beamed to myself. Other passengers noticed my chirpy disposition and I got nods and smiles. I found myself smiling back, without thinking. Even without judgement too. A small step for an ordinary Joe Soap, but a giant leap for Cara Cawley. Smiling at fellow passengers on Dublin Bus. What next? But today, in my vulnerable state, on the cusp of change, I deemed smiling back at strangers a perfectly reasonable way to behave.

Chapter Seven

THE CHAT WITH Doctor Seán, the readjusted
meds and the new self-help book combined to
have a positive impact on my mood over the next
few days. I was sleeping slightly better and had
more energy as a result.

The 'beast within' was being unleashed, slowly
but surely. On Wednesday evening, Declan came
home to find me dancing around the kitchen to
Kate Bush in my underwear. He was horrified!

'Cara, what the hell is going on? What are you
doing?'

'Cloudbusting.'

'What?'

'Look, I'm simply doing some expressive dance.
There's no need to be alarmed.'

'Where's Lucy?'

'In bed.'

'Look, Cara, I'm not sure about any of this.
Why don't you just sit on the couch and listen to
Michael Bublé? Like you used to, with a cup of tea
and a biscuit. Why don't you do that instead of all

this hippy dippy shit?'

'Declan, I've been doing some research lately and I've realised that my self-expression and creativity were trapped inside my body with no means of escape. It's of utmost importance to express myself as much and as often as I can, for my personal development.'

'Your what?'

'A woman of my age, Declan, we are tender, fragile, vulnerable creatures. We need to let go of our inhibitions as often as possible and keep nothing bottled up.'

'Where you getting this info?'

'Elizabeth Gilbert and Angela Paul recommend twenty minutes of freestyle dance every day and...'

'Look, darling, if you want to let go of inhibitions, come down and have a few pints with us in the club! That's what normal people do to let off steam, not dance around the kitchen in their knickers ... ALONE!'

'I didn't think you'd understand. Just forget it, okay?'

'Are you still taking those pills, are you? I think that's why you're acting strange.'

'Yes, I'm taking them, but different ones now. They're making me more stable. Look, the doctor wouldn't have prescribed them if I didn't need them, okay? Just trust that he knows best. I do.'

'When are you going to see him again? I wonder if I should go along with you to give some input?'

'Next week and no, that won't be necessary. I have everything under control.'

'Sure you do,' Declan muttered under his breath. He went to the fridge and took out some leftover chicken and broccoli bake. He heated it in the microwave, while I put my skirt back on and buttoned up my blouse. He mentioned he'd been talking to our neighbour, Bernadette.

'She told me she loved minding Lucy the other day and sounded eager to do it again. She knows you're off sick, so she offered to help out if we ever need her.'

'Really? At her age!' I replied.

'Ah Cara, Bernadette is sprightly. She's a young …' He searched his brain for the right word.

'Senior citizen?' I offered.

'No, no I wasn't going to call her that.'

'Well, that's what she is.'

'She's mature. A mature lady. Anyway, I got to thinking, wouldn't she be a good alternative childminder for Lucy when you go back to work? I mean, Emma's got a long waiting list and Lucy's right at the end of it now. What would you think of Bernadette minding her for a few hours after school?'

'Oh, em, I don't know. She's … It's ….' Just the mention of returning to work quickened my heart rate. I could feel it.

'She's right next door, which would be handy as hell, and Lucy loves both her and her dog, Rex. It's a match made in heaven if you ask me,' declared Declan.

✧   ✧   ✧

OVER THE FOLLOWING days, I couldn't help clocking up a little more debt, but reassured myself it was all for a good cause. Now that I'd discovered the real ME, there was no turning back. That shop between the doctor's surgery and the chemist opened up a whole new world to me. A world of self-help. These books encouraged me to find myself and it turns out I was the perfect age to do just that. Turning forty was a pivotal moment in the life of a female in the twentieth century. I never really understood that my impending birthday could be such a turning point in my life. I wasn't aware until now how much of myself I'd lost since becoming a wife and mother. I listened to Glenn Close's acceptance speech at the Golden Globes over and over again –

> "...women, we're nurturers, that's what's expected of us. We have our children, we have our husbands if we're lucky enough, and our partners. But we have to find personal fulfilment. We have to follow our

dreams. We have to say, 'I can do that, and I should be allowed to do that.'"

This quickly became my mission. Who am I? What was I put on this earth to do? I answered that question straight away—I was meant to have Lucy, I know that much for starters and she's the best thing I've ever done. But what else is meant for me? My mission is incomplete.

I read countless internet articles, bought numerous self-help books aimed at women of my age, listened to a myriad of TedTalks and downloaded self-affirming meditations. Now that I was off the sleeping pills and on the antidepressants instead, I didn't scream out in hallucinatory dreams anymore. Instead, I fell asleep listening to wise gurus repeat how 'abundant' I was and they would sweep me away on guided meditative journeys. I was relieved when I followed these meditations that I was permitted to keep my clothes on, unlike in my previous hallucinatory nightmares. Declan was still upping sticks and leaving to sleep in the spare room. Apparently, he didn't want to chant—

'I am a strong, confident woman. I love my body. I love my shoulders. I love my chest. I love my breasts. I love my tummy. I love my back. I love my pelvis …'

The list was endless, but no, Declan just didn't

seem to get it. He huffed and puffed and pulled the duvet over his head to block out the various hypnotic voices blaring in the bedroom every night. After ten or fifteen minutes, he'd go and remove himself from the bedroom. I wouldn't entertain wearing headphones as he suggested, because I wanted the physical space in the room to be filled with the affirming chants. I didn't feel too guilty when he left the bedroom. We had a Willis and Gambier majestic sleigh-style double bed in the spare room, so I knew he'd be comfortable. This meditative chanting played a major role in discovering my life's purpose, according to my books anyway. It was all on me. I had to be the one to decide what course my life would take and I intended to steer it in my preferred direction.

It was time to check in with the doctor. I had been keeping him updated on my progress over the phone in recent weeks. He told me there was no need to come into the clinic each week, but he would set aside fifteen minutes for a phone consultation with me instead. This cost half the price of a visit to the surgery, so I readily accepted, even though I missed seeing him in person.

I was strangely excited about seeing him for real today. I had enjoyed hearing his voice on the phone each week, but he always sounded so professional and businesslike. I was looking forward to staring into his eyes in his intimate clinic. Despite knowing that I was on an upward trajectory in my recovery, I didn't want to appear too well, in case he would send me back to work. He had been so good at warding off the company doctor up to now.

My boss, Barbara, was loath to pay me sick pay for very much longer. I'd been on full pay for the first month and subsequently half pay. Barbara wanted to cut me off the payroll, unless I got assessed by the company doctor, but my own Doctor Seán intervened and assured her that I was not fit to go back to work any time soon. He told the doctor I wasn't mentally strong enough and that he was still trying to find the right balance of antidepressant medication for me.

The company doctor was content to sign me off for another month on Seán's recommendation, but wished to see me in the near future. She seemed to have a good rapport with Seán, which gave me peace of mind. At least there was a barrier of medics between me and Barbara for the time being and I could hide myself from my boss, for another little while anyway.

I found myself staring at my reflection in the mirror while getting ready for the appointment. I was wearing brand new satin burgundy under-wear, a bra and matching chemise. I had to admit my body was in good shape for someone soon to be entering her fifth decade. I was pale skinned, lightly freckled and mostly hairless. My physique was lean, as I was always on the go, never sitting down long enough to relax. While that wasn't healthy for my mental health, it had granted me a toned, taut figure. I was pleased with my reflection from the neck down.

It was just my face—honestly, I don't remember seeing those three crinkly lines over my left eyebrow this time last month. It's like they appeared out of nowhere to remind me I'm not getting any younger. Is that how a woman's face ages? Lines turn into creases which give way to wrinkles and there's no going back. I raised my brow and it wrinkled more. I scrunched my brow and new lines appeared. The only way I could make those creases invisible was to pull my forehead upwards with my finger, but I couldn't very well walk around like that all day. What would Seán think?

No, no, I vowed, I would find a way to erase those signs of ageing. I made a mental note to do it and a shopping list, before returning to my reflection. I couldn't help but wonder what Seán would make of me now standing here in my lingerie. Would this be enough to turn him on? I was aware he was almost ten years younger than me and in top physical shape, judging by his athletic build and strong frame. I tried to imagine what he would look like standing here beside me in nothing but his underwear. A leery smile crept over my face, as I licked my lips, still staring in the mirror. I assumed, with him being in his prime, he would have his pick of women in their twenties or thirties. His blonde hair flopped loosely to one side and his pale blue eyes were always so attentive and full of concern. Every female patient in that clinic must be madly in love with him.

I wore skin coloured, sheer natural tights with a short black fitted skirt and olive green silk blouse, open a smidgen too low to show off my burgundy undergarments. I knew it was a bit racy with a hint of cleavage, but I didn't care. No one would notice under my coat and I wouldn't take that off until I was safely inside Doctor Seán's intimate consultation room. I wondered if he ever fantasised about me, the way I did about him. I desperately wanted to find out.

I was feeling well enough to drive again. I wore my runners, but brought high heels to change into, as soon as I parked the car. I knew the heels paired with the sheer tights and short skirt would accentuate my long, shapely legs and I felt like showing them off today. I smiled confidently, as I whizzed past the receptionist.

The magazines in the waiting room were of no interest to me now. I didn't need inspiration or advice. I knew what suited me and what didn't. And I knew I looked ravishing today.

'Cara Cawley? You can go in to see Doctor Khan now.'

'What? Who?'

'Doctor Khan will see you now.'

'No! I'm here to see Doctor Seán!'

'Oh, I'm afraid he's on a house call at the moment, but Doctor Khan will see you instead.' The receptionist acted as if this tiny detail was of no consequence.

'A house call? You mean to somebody's home?'

'Yes, one of his elderly patients had a TIA and the family requested Seán, as he's the old man's regular doctor. Just for familiarity, you understand, don't you?'

'Oh, oh I see. I didn't realise he would do home visits.'

'Only in exceptional circumstances. Now Doctor Khan has kindly offered to take his patients while he's away this afternoon.'

'No, that's okay. I'll wait.'

'Oh, but I don't know what time he'll be back! He just left a half an hour ago, he might get stuck in traffic on his way back. You could be waiting hours for him!'

'I'll wait, thank you very much. I want to see my regular doctor, just like the old man.'

The receptionist raised her eyes and called the next patient for Doctor Khan. Then, I started to panic internally, when I realised I wouldn't be home in time to collect Lucy from school. I called Declan.

'Everything okay, Cara? How did you get on at the doctor?'

'Em, well, I'm still here and it looks like I'm going to be waiting a while. It's full up today. Is there any way you can collect Lucy? Maybe take the afternoon off?'

'Ah Cara, I'm in the thick of it now. I can't, I can't get away. There's no way. Can you not tell them you have to collect your daughter from school? Could they make an exception for you?'

'Look Declan, as I said, it's chock-a-block. I can't just skip the queue. What about Emma? Do you think she'd do us a favour just this once?'

'Cara, you don't seem to understand. You took Lucy out of Emma's. She's full up now. We can't get back in and she's too busy to be doing us favours.'

'Damn, why did I do that? Why did you let me?'

'Don't panic, don't panic. Do y'know what? Bernadette, next door, offered to help out with Lucy. Will I ring her and see if she can collect her today? Then, there'll be no rush on you.'

'Lifesaver! Good old Bernadette! Yes, do that. That would be marvellous!'

'Right, right, I'll send you a text, okay? Good luck with the doctor. Ask him when you can get back to work, won't you? They're mad to get you back in the office. They all miss you, Cara. Didn't you read the card that came with the flowers yesterday?'

'Yeah, yeah right. Text me, okay? Bye!' I sighed aloud, oblivious that the other patients had witnessed me blatantly lying to my husband on the phone. I closed my eyes to rationalise the phone call. *I'm merely a patient who wants to see her regular doctor, just like the elderly man that Seán is visiting. It's not my fault he's such a good doctor. He's the only one I trust. Lucy will be fine. Bernadette is reliable.* I thought back to my dear old departed mother's words of wisdom. *'Always tell a lie when the truth doesn't fit in.'* It was perfectly reasonable to concoct a little white lie for Declan. Yes, yes, I reassured myself it was.

Chapter Eight

I SAT BACK on the chair in the waiting room and plugged in my headphones. I listened to a few podcasts first and then chose a guided meditation. I closed my eyes—

'Breathe deeply. Bring your awareness to the ebb and flow of your breath. Let it flow naturally. Each inhale and exhale rhythmically following the last. As you sit there, visualise a grand mountain, where the air is pure and the view is limitless. Be this mountain, and share in its stillness. Grounded in your posture, visualise a lioness climbing upwards to the peak of the mountain. Resolved, determined and graceful. The lioness grounds her body on the summit and looks down upon her kingdom with a proud sense of accomplishment. Be this lioness, and share in her success. Now, keeping your eyes closed and breath steady, picture her prey...'

'Cara Cawley? The doctor will see you now.'

I almost fell off my chair. 'Is it Doctor Seán? Is he back?'

'Yes, you can go in.'

I channelled the lioness, curving my spine as I lifted myself from my station. With a face of determined resolve, I entered the consultation room, eyes narrowed, brow furrowed, ready to pounce on my prey.

'Cara, come in. I'm sorry you had to wait so long. Please, if that ever happens again, feel free to attend one of the other doctors.'

'No, I'd rather see you, Seán.'

'Come in, sit down. You look very ...' He paused while I disrobed, exposing my short skirt and hint of cleavage. '...Eh, healthy,' he finished his sentence. I detected a gulp before he continued. 'How have you been?'

'I've been, em ... I've been on shaky ground, to be honest.'

'Oh? I thought you would have good news for me. How are you responding to the new antidepressants?'

'Hmmm, okay, but I'm still getting used to them. I've had nausea and dizzy spells, but I'm willing to continue giving them a try.'

'And have you been sleeping well?'

'Em, yes. Well, yes and no. No, not really soundly. You know, some nights good, some nights bad.'

'I'm not sure what you mean, Cara. Everyone has good and bad nights. Are you getting roughly six to eight hours most nights? I must say, you look particularly well rested and even glowing.'

'Why, thank you, Seán!' I winked. Oh, Lord above, I actually winked! 'Well, I slept well last night, but prior to that I've been most restless, most restless indeed.'

'Well, I certainly can't write a sick cert for you due to being restless. How is your mental health of late? In our phone consultations, you seemed to be doing all the right things, such as reading self-help books and practising meditation. I commend you for that.'

'Yes, I told you I'm making progress, finding myself, getting mentally stronger, but as far as going back to work, I think that would set me back. I think the panic attacks would return. I still feel vulnerable.'

'Well, physically and mentally, you seem to be progressing superbly and I believe you're fit enough to go back to work. It's time you went to the company doctor, so she can assess you and give you the go ahead to return to employment. I'll make the appointment now.'

His words hit me like a hurley swing to the head. How could he be so clinical? I beseeched him, 'Oh, so you don't want to see me anymore?'

'Cara, this is a good thing! I think you're no longer in a fragile state. You're doing well, I can tell. I'm going to let the company doctor know that, in my opinion, you'll be fit to return to work in one week. That's enough time for her to assess you and if she agrees, then your life can return to normal. That's good news, isn't it?'

'Oh,' I replied, downcast. The hurley swung at me again, this time pounding me in the heart. Ouch.

I was beginning to get tired. After all, I'd been at the surgery most of the afternoon waiting for him, and now this. Goodbye, good riddance, you're discharged. It felt all wrong. This was not what I'd planned. Seán came out from behind his desk to wish me luck, but I couldn't bear it, so I raced out the door.

I bundled myself into my car, totally forgetting to take off the high heels and change into my runners. I left the car park and spotted a diner down the road. It occurred to me that I hadn't had any lunch and was starving, so I pulled in. I quickly texted Declan to let him know that I'd be late home, and promptly ordered a burger, chips and salad. I reached into my handbag and took out my latest book—*How To Get More Than You Give*. Ha! So much for that, I thought. I got nothing today and he says my life can go back to normal. I wiped a tear from my eye when no one was looking. And then, boom! Who walked in, only Doctor Seán himself! We immediately met each other's eyes and there was an awkward pause. He seemed uncomfortable and looked away.

'Seán! Seán!' I bellowed. 'Please, come over, join me.' I imagine my exuberance made it awkward for him to refuse. That's what I was going for anyway. He hesitated by the counter, but decided to accept my invitation. I guess he had no choice.

'Hi, I didn't get a chance to get lunch today. This place has a great burger,' he said.

'Oh, great! That's exactly what I ordered!' We met eyes briefly and smiled. I couldn't remember ever being so happy.

'So, do you come here often?' I hastily enquired. When we both registered the clichéd chat-up line, we laughed.

'Em, yeah I do actually. It's a handy stop off on my way home and I'm never disappointed with the food. Have you been here before?'

'No, but like you, I also got no lunch. I spotted the flashing "open" sign and pulled in. I … ah, I discovered the shop beside your clinic recently, Word Haven. I absolutely love it! Have you been inside?'

'Oh yeah, I often pop in on my lunch break. It's fantastic! Not your run-of-the-mill bookshop, sure it isn't? It's got a lot of new age stuff and alternative music. I'm glad you discovered it too.' We nodded our heads in total agreement. *Soooooo exciting!*

Seán ordered a burger and we ate, conversed and laughed. To all present, it must have seemed as though we were on a date, but to us, we were parting ways as doctor and patient, and getting to know each other over a burger. The meal continued with no awkwardness, both of us eager to get to know each other and sharing a mutual appreciation of the food.

The last salty chip had been consumed and the diner was filling up with Friday evening customers. It was already dark outside. Seán made the first move to go.

'Well, Cara, thanks for your company. I'm usually quite the loner in here, always in a rush after work. I'm sure the staff must think me an oddball!'

'Oh, I doubt that. I bet they're delighted you enjoy the food so much and now you've gained a new customer for them! I'll definitely be back!'

'Oh great! No doubt your husband and daughter would love it too!'

My smile faded immediately and it didn't go unnoticed.

'Oh sorry, Cara, have I said the wrong thing?'

I didn't want him ruining the best date of my life. I wanted to live in the moment a little longer.

This idea just sprang to mind. Totally last minute. 'No, it's not your fault. It's just me and Declan, we've … split up.'

'Oh! I didn't know! I'm sorry.'

'No, no, you weren't to know. But I'm glad it came out. Now you know that I'm single.'

A slightly awkward silence followed.

'Well, I imagine this is a very recent split. Must be still raw…'

'No, no not at all! I'm completely over it. It was my choice, actually.'

'And how is Lucy? Is she taking it okay?'

'Em, oh Lucy, yes, good question. She, eh … well you know, em, kids, they're, em, very resilient,' I announced, while my watering eyes caught me by surprise with their perfect timing and heartfelt emotion. God, I was good. Nothing I couldn't put my hand to. Even at the ripe old age of thirty-nine, I was still impressing myself on a regular basis.

Seán reached out his hand to shake mine. 'You take care of yourself, Cara. The company doctor will liaise with me during the week about your return to work.'

'I wonder what I'll do with Lucy when I go back to work. If I had an extra week or two, I'd have time to work out a timetable with my ex-husband, you know.' I searched him pleadingly and put on my best puppy dog eyes expression.

'Yes, right, well, as I said, I'll liaise with the company doctor. I'll do what I can for you, Cara, okay?'

This time I grabbed his hand and squeezed it. 'Yes, yes, I know you will. Thanks, Seán, thanks for everything.'

He glanced away shyly, nodded his head and walked away.

'Seán?' I called.

He turned around. 'Yes?'

'Hope to see you here again sometime?'

'Oh, sure, yeah. Bye now.'

I congratulated myself. That was a perfectly reasonable, casual way to secure a further date with the little darling!

Chapter Nine

LATER THAT EVENING, I floated in the front door as if walking on air. I felt jazz hands waving through my bloodstream, with the touch of Seán's hand still palpable on my skin. I burst through the living room door to find Declan engrossed in *GAA Giants* on RTE1.

'Hellooooo, Declan!' I swung my arms high in the air, allowing my hips sway side to side.

'What? What are you on now?' Declan was aghast. He paused the programme.

'Nothing! I'm just high on life, Deckie Boy!' I winked, for the second time that day.

'Are you drunk, or what?'

'Ah hahahahahahaha...!' I cackled. 'Can't a woman simply beam from her innards out, without being drunk?'

'Innards?'

'I feel like dancing! Can I put on some music, Declan? Let's dance!'

'Cara, how did you get on at the doctor? Sit down for a minute and tell me.'

'Oh, Doctor Seán is AMAZING! He's sooooo … attentive!'

'I'm not asking about HIM, for Christ's sake! I'm asking about YOU! How did YOU get on?'

'Marvellous! Just swimmingly, thanks!'

'OK, that's better than I expected. So, back to work on Monday?'

'Hmmmm? What? Work?'

'Yes, did he say you were fit to go back?'

'Oh, well now, Declan, steady on! Don't jump the gun! You can't rush these things you know.'

'Rush these things? Rush these things! Cara, you've been off work for over two months! You're down to half pay for the last four weeks and they're threatening not to pay you if the sick leave continues! We need your income. You know how tight things are! I'm taking all the overtime I can get, but we still need a second income.'

'They won't cut my pay, Declan. I'll make sure of that.'

'So, what did he say? Are you going back to work or what?'

'He has referred me to the company doctor and she will deem me fit or not to go back. I've an appointment with her on Tuesday morning, so I'll know more then.'

'Good, that's good. That's progress anyway. What about your medication?'

'No change. The antidepressants are working

well.'

'Will you be on them forever?'

'No, just a few months. I'm not ready to come off them yet. Give me time.'

'Yeah, yeah, your mood has definitely improved, to say the least! Oh yeah, Lucy got on great with Bernadette this afternoon. I had to work late, so Bernadette kept her until seven o'clock. I told her we'd fix up with her, but she insisted it was "her pleasure" and that Lucy is great company for her.'

'Brilliant! I'm sure Lucy had a ball. She loves playing with Rex, doesn't she?'

'Yeah, yeah she does! I wanted to talk to you about Bernadette. I was wondering should we ask her to be Lucy's childminder when you go back to work? We'd pay her and the drop-off and collection would be so simple, with her being next door. She could walk Lucy to school and collect her and she has the car anyway for rainy days. What do you think? She was a godsend today.'

'Yeah, it would be handy alright. I wonder, would Lucy be a bit lonely, though. She was used to playing with other children at the childminder's.'

'Well, she could still go on a playdate once or twice a week. I'm sure Bernadette would drop her off for an hour here and there. She'd give her a snack after school, they could walk the dog, do some homework and watch a cartoon or two. Sure they'd fill their time, no bother. I'd say Bernadette would sit down with her and play. She's that type of person, y'know?'

'I play with Lucy! We did our structured play-time for one point five hours every second day of the week when I was off ...'

'I didn't mean that! I wasn't getting at you, okay? I just meant that I think she has everything we would want in a childminder for Lucy. I mean, why didn't we think of it before?'

'Yes, okay, I'll consider it, but we don't need her yet. I'm not back at work yet, am I? We'll see how I get on at the doctor on Tuesday. Now, a cup of chamomile. Do you want a cup of tea?'

'Don't feel like dancing anymore, do you?'

I felt heat in my cheeks. 'Em, no. No, I don't know what I was thinking.'

'So, where are your bags?'

'My what?'

'You were shopping, weren't you? Did you buy anything?'

'Oh!' I'd forgotten I texted him that so I could stay on a bit longer with Seán in the diner. Just a little white lie, that's all it was. Mother would approve. 'No, no I only browsed this evening. The stuff is cheaper online anyway.'

Declan nodded and pressed play. *GAA Giants* promptly resumed.

✧ ✧ ✧

THE NEXT MORNING, I took Lucy to the park bright and early. She wanted to try cycling without her training wheels. I thought she was too young, but Declan took them off before putting the bike in the car. It was one of those crisp, fresh mornings with a clear, blue sky. I was surprised to see so many people in the park. Mainly families with young children, kicking a ball, scooting or making their way to the playground. I was impressed by the amount of joggers too. Hmmm, everyone's so fit and healthy, I observed.

Lucy was determined to move onto the next stage of bike riding today. 'Grace and Zoe cycled to school last week with NO training wheels,' she insisted. There was a competitive streak in her, probably from her Daddy. She mounted her little bike and could reach the pavement either side with her tippy toes.

'Let's go, Mommy!' she beamed. 'You run along beside me, okay? In case I fall, okay?'

'Yes, darling, I'll be right beside you, I promise.'

Lucy actually surprised me. She wobbled a little in the beginning, but got straight back on. She had no fear, it seemed. It wasn't long before I was out of breath trying to keep up with her zipping along on her bike. I noticed a jogger in the distance. His build and frame caught my attention. It looked uncannily like Seán. Could it be him?

In one way, I hoped it was, as I'd love to bump into him unexpectedly, but in another way, I was wearing jeans and runners and no mascara. I certainly wasn't looking my best, so maybe I should keep a low profile. I was so distracted that I didn't notice a dog ahead of me had broken free of its lead. Before I knew it, I got tangled in the dog's fallen lead and went flying to the ground. Lucy also got a fright, swerved and hit the ground too. We both screamed in unison. Passersby rushed to our aid.

I had gone down, face first, with my arms outstretched in Lucy's direction as a last-minute attempt to protect her. It was my face and left arm that took the hit. I could barely move my arm in fact, but ignored the pain momentarily to check Lucy, who was still bawling. An elderly lady picked up her bike and made reassuring noises that she was a brave girl. It seemed Lucy got away with just grass stains, as her bike had swerved to the right, away from the path and onto the grass.

I wasn't so lucky, however, and the pain was excruciating. I couldn't move my arm and blood was running down the side of my face. Lucy was horrified at the sight of me. 'MOMMY! MOMMY!' she yelled. I allowed the mortified dog owner to help me up into a sitting position and reached into my pocket for my phone with my one good arm. I imagined Declan would be kitted out and ready to take to the pitch right about now.

'She fell off her bike? Is she okay?' he asked.

'Yes, she just got a fright, that's all. But, I fell too. I tripped over a dog's lead and went flying. Ahhh …' I groaned in pain.

'What? Is this a joke, Cara? I'm playing a match now!'

'No, no you're not, Declan. I can't move my arm. I need to go to the hospital right this second! Come and get us.'

The owner of the escaped dog went to the ice cream van and bought Lucy a 99, while we waited for Declan.

✧　✧　✧

A&E WAS TRYING. I was wincing in pain by the time we got there. However, we had no choice but to wait. Declan left me on my own for a while, when he dropped Lucy to his mother's. When he got back to the hospital, I was still waiting to be seen. I was crying in pain and he rubbed my back in an attempt to comfort me. He didn't know what else to do. Another hour went by and his phone rang.

'Jim, it's a joke here. She hasn't even been seen yet. The place is chock-a-block!'

'Ah yeah, I suppose, Saturday afternoon. Always accidents on a Saturday, you're right there, Jim.'

I couldn't hear Jim on the line, only Declan's replies, but tried to piece together his questions nonetheless.

'Well, she couldn't move her arm, so we knew straight away it was broken. She was running along with Lucy on her bike. She didn't take her eyes off her for a second she said, and this dog ran straight into her with a long lead trailing behind it. Cara got tangled in the lead and went flying.'

'What's that, Jim? Oh, yeah, lucky to get away with just a broken arm, yeah, I suppose you're right.'

'Although, now that you mention it, she's sitting here beside me and half her face is covered in scratches and cuts. It'll bruise up nicely in a couple of days, no doubt. It's all superficial though, I'd say. Poor thing, she looks like she got into a brawl in a nightclub or something.'

'A photo?' He looked my way and I mouthed 'no way.'

'What's that? Why didn't she put her hands out to protect her face? Sure, she was far too busy looking after Lucy, apparently. She only had eyes for her.' I put my head down and touched my forehead with my good hand when he said that. A shot of pain ran through my brain. Or was it guilt?

'Ah yeah, Jim. A completely selfless act to put herself in the line of fire. All to protect young Lucy. Indeed you're right, Jim, a perfectly reasonable thing to do. I'll pass on your regards.'

Chapter Ten

I WAS DOSED up on painkillers all of Sunday and Monday. I was so grateful to Cathy, my mother-in-law, and Bernadette, next door, for sharing the minding of Lucy.

I lay in bed on Tuesday morning thinking about the accident. The image of the jogger came to mind. I was sure it had been Seán. I'd been so distracted trying to figure out whether it was him or not that I took my eye off Lucy and wasn't even watching where I was going either. *Am I a woman deranged?* Was my infatuation with Seán turning into an obsession?

I found it hard to believe that I fractured my arm and smashed up my face because I thought I saw my doctor jogging way off in the distance. *Oh God, I must be going mad!* Poor Lucy, getting such a fright too. Thank God, she was okay. *I'm such a bad mother. I need to take action and get back to where I was before all this depression and obsession took over my life.*

I hauled myself out of bed with great difficulty,

dosed myself up on painkillers and struggled to get dressed. There would be no glamour today for the company doctor. I managed jeans, runners and a loose sweatshirt. I looked in the mirror and realised there was no point in applying makeup. I looked hideous, but there was no chance makeup would cover up any of my lesions. I dabbed around the open wounds with some ointment and was relieved, mainly for Lucy's sake, that the worst of the cuts around the side of my face were covered with plasters. I made some coffee and toast and headed down to the bus stop. I wouldn't be able to drive again until my arm was better.

People at the bus stop were so nice to me. 'What happened?' an old lady enquired. I relayed my version of events and was rewarded with heartfelt sympathy and a pat on the shoulder. Why was I previously so critical about people taking public transport? *I'm lucky to be able to travel on the bus with them. Can't exactly afford taxi fares to cart me around anyway.*

I was grateful the bus driver waited for me to sit down before pulling off. I must have looked quite a wreck to warrant such special treatment. I put my hand to my nose to acclimatise to that bus smell and looked out the window.

Dublin city was spreading out. I passed so many new blocks of apartments and townhouses being erected on the outskirts of the city. Scaffolding and construction work hid the landscape from my fleeting eye. It seemed there was a huge demand to live within a LUAS ride or walking distance to the city centre. I could understand the appeal with so many galleries, museums, restaurants, pubs and high street shopping on your doorstep. If I was childless and single, I would want to live in one of the new apartments I'd spotted, but the suburbs suited family life much better. Lucy and Declan needed the long back garden to let off some steam. They'd never survive in a gated compound with a tiny balcony or miniature terrace.

It wasn't long before I felt a sense of doom rising from the pit of my stomach. I couldn't believe I had to actually go into the office to see the company doctor. It was unfair to march sick people through the office, only to be surveyed by the nosey employees. There should be a separate clinic for the doctor to occupy, but she used a meeting room to assess patients, which of course, happened to be on my floor.

My breathing quickened as the bus slowed down. My mind raced. This was a bloody disaster. I was completely unprepared for the looming consultation. I thought of Seán. I should have gone to HIM this morning. He could have protected me from this encounter. He could have liaised with the company doctor, as he had done previously. I reached my destination, pressed the red button and disembarked.

Panic set in as I approached the revolving door. I tried taking deep breaths when the mat got stuck, but it was impossible to catch my breath. Nevertheless, I persevered and tried to control it. I yanked at the mat until the door moved again. I continued to strive for deep breaths in the lift on the way up to the second floor, to no avail. My breathing took off on its own, a separate entity now, and I could feel my mind wandering away too. I should have taken a benzo this morning. I berated myself and my lack of preparation.

The lift door opened and I had to force my body out. Kate noticed my arrival through the main door and rushed over.

'Cara! Oh my God, Cara, what happened? Were you in an accident?'

I froze and then remembered what a monstrosity I must have looked.

'Em, yes, of sorts.'

Suddenly, others rushed over and I was surrounded. No one knew what to say. The most they could manage was an awkward, insincere, 'Cara, good to see you back.'

I just stared back blankly at them, thinking, no ... no, it isn't, you bare-faced liars! No one's happy to see me back and I'm raging I had to set foot in the door!

The crowd dispersed as it was obvious I was not in the mood for small talk. Barbara appeared and offered to escort me to the doctor, being the 'saint' that she was. We walked together past gawking faces.

'Oh Cara, we've all been so worried about you. Did you get the flowers?'

'Yes ... thanks.'

Barbara was happy to keep our conversation to a minimum, so she knocked on the doctor's door and poked her head in.

'Hi Linda, Cara Cawley is here. You were expecting her?'

'Yes, thanks Barbara. Come in Cara, take a seat. Oh! What happened to you?' She looked horrified.

I sat down and nodded to Barbara as she took her leave. Barbara's fake show of concern presented my racing mind with a new idea.

'Hi Doctor, I'm depressed and have been for months now. I find I get so down that I regularly consider self harming. You see this?' I pointed to my face and arm. 'I did this to myself. I maimed myself. I deliberately injured myself as punishment for being depressed. Is this normal, Doctor?'

'When, em, when did you do this to yourself?'

'Saturday. I threw myself down, face first on the pavement. I had practised this before, but never managed to sustain a proper injury. I must be getting good at it though, because this time I broke my arm in two places. The scars on my face are just an added bonus. It was the first time I fell like that.'

'Cara, this is very serious. Have you ever tried to self-harm before?'

Briefly, I harped back to my mother's advice, regarding truth. And lies. I decided a little lie would give me a much needed boost right now.

'The odd prick with a knife to score blood, but other than that, no.'

'Have you told your GP?'

'No, but I did mention the depression, not the self-harm.'

'I see. Would you mind undressing? I'd like to have a look at your body?'

The doctor helped me undress and noted the bruises on my left leg due to my recent fall. She helped me back on with my clothes and I requested to use the bathroom to fix myself up. There was a door in her consultation room, which led to the corridor where the bathroom was. However, as I left, my heart jumped when I heard the mention of Seán's name. Linda was ringing him. I decided there and then not to bother with the bathroom. I could fix myself up later. I made noise as if I was on my way, but tiptoed back to her door as softly as I could. I pushed it out ever so slightly, in order to eavesdrop without being noticed. It was so quiet, I could hear his pleading voice on the line.

'Linda, believe me! I didn't know she was self-harming. That never came up in our consultations, even the ones over the phone. She never mentioned it.'

'Seán, it's very rare that the patient will offer this information. It's up to you to probe her and draw it out of her. Did you ever examine her body and look for marks?'

'No, but there didn't seem to be any need for that. If I had thought …'

'But you knew she was having dark, depressive thoughts. I read it in her chart. And it didn't cross your mind that she might self-harm? You should see her now, Seán. She's on the edge, extremely fragile and desperately unstable.'

'I'm just so surprised by this turnaround. When I saw her on Friday night, she seemed so jovial and together.'

'Friday night? Have you been seeing this woman outside of surgery hours?'

'Oh, no, well not intentionally. I bumped into her at the local diner and we had dinner there.' My heart was beating so fast now, I really hoped she wouldn't hear it. I tried my hardest to stay still.

'Are you seriously telling me you had a dinner date with one of the most unstable patients I've ever observed?' Ouch, that hurt. I didn't think my acting skills were that good.

'It was a purely accidental meeting, I can assure you. And she definitely didn't seem unstable. Well, apart from admitting she was going through a separation.'

'Oh, she didn't mention that today.'

'Well, you sometimes have to elicit this information from a patient, Linda.' Oooh, he was getting cheeky now. I loved it!

'Seán, please don't get smart with me, okay? I have grave concerns about this lady and I just can't fathom how you thought her fit enough to resume employment!'

'Look, you said it yourself, she had a fall. Whether it was intended or accidental, I don't know, but maybe this set her back. I'm not lying when I tell you she progressed well on the medication and other wellbeing exercises she was trying out. She was far from the woman I encountered a few months ago on the verge of a nervous breakdown. Her confidence and self-esteem had notably improved and she looked to be on top of her mental health.'

Then, Linda whispered. 'Fit enough to take out to dinner, was she?'

'That's not fair, Linda!' he retorted.

'Right, I'll put her on strong pain relief for her facial wounds and broken arm. She's still taking the anti-depressants and she should have some benzodiazepine left over, from what I see in her prescription. That will do until I see her next week. I think it's best if I take over as her main practitioner now. Do you agree?' My heart sank.

'Well, I suppose I don't have much choice, do I? I more or less discharged her anyway when I referred her to you. Things are hectic down here, so I guess one less patient on the books will lighten the load.'

'Really? Is that how you feel?' Linda was quick off the mark.

'Oh, oh no, I didn't mean it that way. I wouldn't just ...'

'Just what? Discharge someone too early to lighten the workload?'

'You know I would never intentionally do that. You know that, Linda!'

'Send me Mrs Cawley's file, Seán. I'll be in touch if I have any more queries.' She hung up. I made some shuffling noises then, to warn her I was finished and on my way back. I sat down opposite her with my very best, most innocent expression.

'Cara, I really wasn't expecting to see you like this. During my last conversation with Seán, he thought your mood had improved and noted a decrease in your anxiety levels. He seemed to believe the anti-depressants were agreeing with you and you would be fit to return to work.'

I beamed maniacally and gave a thumbs up with my right arm. I didn't mind hanging him now. He didn't fight for me. He didn't try hard enough to keep me as his patient.

'Oh, wonderful! That's just hunky dory! When do I start back?'

Doctor Linda paused and looked alarmed.

'Who treated your injuries, Cara? It wasn't Seán, or he would have let me know.'

'I went to A&E in the Merryfield Hospital.'

'Okay, I need to touch base with the hospital and check through your records. I'm going to recommend you stay off work at half pay for a further month. I'm also going to research treatment possibilities for you. I'd like to see you again next week, back here at the same time. Do you understand, Mrs Cawley?'

'Yes. May I go now? There's a bus leaving in ten minutes.'

I exited the office with my head held high, congratulating myself along the way for being so resourceful. My somewhat disturbing, wide-eyed smile didn't go unnoticed by my colleagues and I sensed the eerie chill it sent up their spines. I congratulated myself a second time for this!

Declan had arranged for Bernadette to collect Lucy from school until the cuts on my face were less visible. I couldn't be scaring all the little children with my injuries, he'd insisted. With that, I took more pain relief, popped one of my last remaining benzos and lay on the couch pondering all the wonderful things I could get up to in the coming month.

Christmas was almost upon us and the office would be closed for a week. I realised with the few days this week added to the month and the extra week off for the silly season, I had almost six weeks of leisure time to look forward to. Yes! That was a perfectly reasonable amount of time for me to make a full recovery. And then some…

Chapter Eleven

HOUSEWORK WAS PROVING arduous with only one arm. I attempted to dust our made-to-measure real wooden Venetian blinds from Hillarys, but got distracted when I overheard Declan's voice through the open window.

'Ah God, Bernadette, are you sure? You've had her all day! Don't you need a break?'

'Declan, I promise you, Lucy is no trouble at all. She's a little angel in fact, as well you know! Leave her here with me for another few hours. You go to the club and do your training session. Let Cara rest herself after that terrible accident, the poor dear. Lucy and I will be just fine,' she reassured him with her soothing voice.

This is great, I thought. She loves minding Lucy and is refusing any payment so far. Declan was right about this. I had a nice rest, as Bernadette advised, and then collected Lucy, who was worn out from playing with Rex. She fell asleep in record time and as I was opening her blinds a smidgen to let some light in for the morning, I heard Declan's car pull in the driveway. Lucy liked going to sleep with the blackout blinds shut tight, but hated waking up in a darkened room, so I always loosened them slightly to allow a glimmer of light in before she awoke.

I peeped out the window and noticed Declan holding a large bunch of flowers in his arms as he got out of the car. *I'll kill him!* I told him not to waste our money on... But he didn't come to our front door. He hopped over the wall and approached Bernadette's front door. Hmmm, payment in flowers. That won't last. I knew I was turning into a Nosey Ninney of late, but I went to the spare room, as it was closer to Bernadette's, and opened the window to hear him deliver the flowers. I was just in time.

'Oh Declan! I don't know what to say! They're beautiful! It's been a long time since someone bought me flowers, you know!' I raised my eyes, cringing for both of them.

'Ah Bernadette, you've been so good to us and you won't take a penny for it. At least take these as a token of our appreciation.' Ah, he's right. I married a very kind-hearted man. I was aware I took him for granted, at times.

'I accept! Thank you, Declan, but there really was no need.'

'There's a fine smell running through your hallway, Bernadette. Sausages, is it?'

'Oh lord, thank you for reminding me! They're on the pan, sizzling away. Will you come in, Declan?'

I walked away. I knew what his answer would be. There was no way he'd refuse a fried sausage.

It was after ten o'clock when he finally arrived home. I called him from upstairs.

'Why were you so long?'

'I went into Bernadette's thinking Lucy was still there and she had sausages on the pan. Then *GAA Giants* was starting, so we watched that. Why? What's wrong? I thought you'd be asleep.'

'I would be if I could. I can't get comfortable in bed. I need to be knocked out if I'm gonna sleep. Did you hide any of those sleeping pills I used to take? I thought there was one or two left before I changed medication, but I can't find them anywhere.'

'Ah no, not the ones that make you go loopy? Sure, no one in the house will get any sleep if you're taking them again!'

'Declan, just one, please! I'm really suffering. I can't even lie on my left side with the pain. It would knock me out, just one, I know it would.'

'Yeah, of course I hid the damn things. I had to. You were screaming half the night like a lunatic, you were! I'll get one now for you, but just the one, okay?'

'Yeah, that's all I want, thanks, Declan.'

He studied my smashed up face as he handed me the pill. The bruises were coming out now in a variety of shades. Between the cuts, plasters and my arm in the cast, he knew I was in dire pain. He admitted that he couldn't begrudge me one lousy sleeping pill in my hour of need. I was grateful and let him kiss me on the side of my mouth that wasn't cut.

✧   ✧   ✧

THE BRUISING CAME out in all its glory over the next few days. While the cuts slowly healed and the plasters were removed, my face turned a multicoloured shade of yellow and purple. I still couldn't be seen outdoors, except for absolute necessities, like my impending Tuesday morning appointment in the office with Doctor Linda. I'd had a whole week of lounging indoors to think about the way I would play this one. No elaborate plan was concocted though, as I felt I functioned better thinking on my feet and an idea would probably form in my mind as soon as I entered the office.

I'd had no real contact with the outside world all week, no phone calls from the office, no enquiries from the doctor or no concerned messages from the people I used to consider my friends. I realised I hadn't made much of an effort with anyone in recent years, so it didn't come as much of a surprise that my friendships had, for the most part, fizzled out. I spoke with Cathy over the phone, one call from Jim's wife, Claire, when she called out of the blue and of course, I had contact with Bernadette next door. Lucy got used to her mommy's injuries after the initial shock, and obviously Declan was my main point of contact with the outside world.

I spent much of my downtime alone and longed for the day when I could dress up, wear makeup and orchestrate a chance meeting with Seán. I missed having him in my life and imagined from our last romantic encounter in the diner that he might be missing me too. The way he had looked at me that evening. I yearned for his eyes to examine me all over again.

With my time off, I managed to plan our next rendezvous from start to finish in my head. It would be in the book shop next to the clinic, or the diner where we had the Friday night meal. I remembered he had casually mentioned that he often ends up there after work or, failing that, he occasionally pops into the book store during his lunch break. I had ample time to fantasise about our meeting. Of course, I would no longer have my cast and the scarring would be completely erased from my face. Obviously, my hair would be perfectly blow-dried too. I'd be wearing that short, tight, black skirt again, as I remembered how Seán's eyes had lowered a few times to steal a glimpse of my figure. How I wished he was still my GP instead of the conscientious, fresh-faced, diligent Doctor Linda.

✧　✧　✧

TUESDAY MORNING ARRIVED quicker than I would have liked. I put some concealer over my bruises, but it didn't really hide them. How was I going to play this? I knew I had sick leave secured until after Christmas, so no extra time was required at this point. Although, it would be great to get referred back to Doctor Seán, and I wondered if there was any way of wrangling that.

Another glorious bus journey into the office, where everyone was so kind and friendly and helpful. Most people didn't seem bothered about my smashed up face. Sure, they'd most likely seen a lot worse on public transport. It gave me a slight boost about my appearance, until I walked into the office and immediately felt all eyes on me. I received a guarded greeting from my co-workers. Kate and Barbara came over with welcoming smiles on their faces. I wondered how much they knew, but then remembered the doctor confidentiality code and felt more at ease.

'Hi Cara, you look … you look … a lot better

than last week! How are you feeling?' Kate enquired.

'Yes, a little better, thanks. How's everything here?'

'Oh you know, busy as ever. We're all putting in extra hours now to get everything in order before Christmas. We're just dying for the week off!' Barbara enthused.

I attempted a smile, but found I couldn't quite squeeze one out. Barbara rescued me. 'Well, Cara, I wish you well in your recovery and we look forward to having you back on board with us early in the new year!'

'Yes, yes, I hope I'll be well enough to return. I better, em...'

'Oh yes, the doctor's expecting you. Good luck!' I felt Barbara was halfhearted in her wishes, but I could have been wrong. I carried on towards the wide open door.

Linda was sitting behind her desk, fresh-faced and professional as usual.

'Good morning, Cara!' she exclaimed. 'Ah, I see your bruises are out in full show, but that's a good thing. They won't last long. Another week and they'll barely be noticeable.'

'Oh good, I'll be able to show my face again,' I acknowledged.

'Oh, I hope you haven't been cooped up in the house all week? Have you been getting any fresh air?'

'No, not much, but I plan to get out and about as soon as my face improves.'

'Good! And how is your arm?' She seemed so concerned, like a perfect doctor, in fact.

'I'm due back at the hospital tomorrow for a check-up. I've been managing okay, apart from having difficulty getting comfortable in bed. I can still cook though, with one arm, and do light housework, but I miss driving.'

'Yes, of course. I'm afraid you'll most likely be in the cast for another five or six weeks at least. It's a good thing you're right-handed! Are you managing your pain?'

'Yes, I'm taking pain relief every day and I think they'll give me more at my appointment tomorrow. I've no more benzos left at this stage, but I'm still on the anti depressants. I don't want to come off them.'

'No, not at all. You're managing well on them. I spoke to Doctor Dempsey and …'

'Oh, how is he? How is Seán?' My heart did a somersault.

'He's fine. They're very busy in that clinic on the MacMillan Road.'

'Yes, I know. Was he asking for me?'

'Yes, well, that's why I made contact, so he could transfer your file history to me.'

I sank back into my chair and felt my shoulders

drop.

'Is there a problem, Cara?'

'No, no, I just miss Seán, that's all. I miss him … Doctor Seán.'

'Look, if there's anything you want to talk about, you can discuss it with me, you know.'

'Yes, yes, I just felt so comfortable with him. We had formed a bond over the past few months and …'

'Well, you know the doctor/patient "bond" as you say, is a professional one. You do understand that, Cara?'

'Hmmmm? Oh yes, we had a very above board, proper relationship.'

'Relationship?'

'I mean, doctor/patient relationship.'

'Oh, I see,' Linda replied while scribbling ferociously.

'Now, Cara, I'll check your blood pressure and I expect they will do a more thorough examination at the hospital tomorrow.'

I PICKED UP a few bits and pieces for Lucy in town. I felt well after the doctor's visit. It wasn't half as painful as I'd imagined. I held a slight sense of elation in my heart with the thought that Seán had been discussing me with Linda. I was still on his mind, I reassured myself, even if it was just in a professional capacity.

When I arrived home, I collected Lucy from Bernadette's. Good old Bernadette was always on for a chat. That woman craved company since her husband passed away. I wasn't really in the mood for a cuppa though, so I feigned a headache and brought Lucy home. I was tired after my first day out in a long time and decided on an early night.

I heard Declan's key in the door after eleven o'clock. Probably another session at the club that he forgot to tell me about. I wasn't in the mood to hear all the latest gossip. It was always the same old useless information about someone I hardly knew and it made no difference to my life, yet Declan loved to share the news with me. He seemed to believe he was keeping me in the loop by feeding me the latest updates. Well, no thank you, not tonight. I'm not interested, I muttered to myself, as I rolled over and fell asleep, thinking what a perfectly reasonable thing it was to do in my delicate condition.

Chapter Twelve

THE NEXT MORNING over coffee, I asked Declan where he'd been the night before.

'I heard you come in around eleven, but I was exhausted.'

'Bernadette invited me in for a few sausages. She's eh ...'

'Lonely, yes I know. Were you eating sausages until eleven o'clock?'

'Ah well, she had a few cans of Guinness in the fridge and we watched *GAA Giants* and ...'

'So, what? You had a "session" with Bernadette?'

'Not a session, only a couple of cans. Then, herself and Lucy had baked cakes earlier that day, so we had a few slices.'

'*GAA Giants* finishes at ten, doesn't it?'

'We've a lot in common, Cara. She remembers all the old players from Wexford, you know the team in the 1950's that ...'

'Oh, is that her era? Hahaha!'

'Hardly, she's sprightly, she is. Knows all about

the historic players and ...'

'Yeah, I get it. You've a lot in common.'

'We do and I'm very grateful to her for minding Lucy so well. She said you wouldn't have a cup of tea with her yesterday.'

'I had a headache, Declan. Anyway, I'm not her carer.'

'Jeez, that's harsh, Cara. You've become very cynical ever since you started on that medication.'

'I thought you thought I was always cynical?'

'Well, this is a new level of cynicism, picking on our kind, generous neighbour.'

'Alright, alright, I'll have a cup of tea with her next time, okay?'

He downed the rest of his coffee and left for work. I breathed a sigh of relief when he drove off. What was happening to us? We couldn't seem to converse anymore without rubbing each other up the wrong way. I wondered if he was right. Had my personality changed since I went on the meds? I made a mental note to check with Linda if that's a possible side effect.

✧ ✧ ✧

MY FACE IMPROVED over the next few days. I even thought I looked decent enough to bring Lucy to Declan's weekend match, but was told I was off the hook. Bernadette had offered to bring her along, and Declan accepted without even asking me. I observed them in the front garden organising their packed lunch.

'Cheese and ham, cheese and egg, plain cheese or jam.'

'And what's that one?'

'Oh, that's a breakfast roll with rasher, sausage and ...'

'Magic! I'll have that!'

'Of course you will, Declan. I made that one especially for you and the plain cheese ones are for Lucy. I'll have the cheese and ham and we'll share the rest.'

'Ah, you're a star, Bernadette. They'll all really appreciate that at the club, they will.'

I got bored of all the heartfelt appreciation, so I wished them luck and went back inside. I was actually starting to feel left out of my own family circle now. Maybe this was how Declan felt back when I was breastfeeding Lucy. Perhaps I did push him away a bit.

I heard the car pull out of the driveway. Bernadette seemed to be much more sociable and generous than me, making sandwiches to share around. I never did that. She also seemed excited about going to the match. I'd always dreaded it and searched for any excuse under the sun not to go. Obviously, she had way more in common with my husband than I did.

✧ ✧ ✧

MY APPEARANCE IMPROVED and I found I could wear makeup again to conceal any blemishes left on my face. Life ticked on in the Cawley household relatively smoothly, apart from my niggling, ongoing desire to see Seán again. It was as if we had unfinished business to attend to. I knew I couldn't just rock up in his clinic, as he had transferred my records over to Linda, but I still remembered where he liked to eat a quick bite after work or where he enjoyed browsing for books at lunch time.

I organised Bernadette to look after Lucy and hopped on the bus to make my way to the bookshop, just on the off chance that Seán would drop in on his lunch hour. I flicked through magazines and stood by the window, hoping he would pop outside for some fresh air. Alas, no sign of him.

It was two-thirty when I left the bookshop and made my way to the diner with a couple of magazines. I ordered a coffee and scone, as I didn't want to ruin my appetite in case he popped in after work. I'd love it if he joined me for another burger and my mouth watered at the thoughts of it. Surgery ended at four-thirty, but I knew he could still be seeing patients far beyond that time. I ordered more coffee and waited.

By six o'clock I realised he must have left the surgery and be on his way. I waited another half-hour just in case he'd pop in, but still there was no sign of him.

Damn it, I thought to myself, I'm wasting my time here. I should have waited near the clinic to see him get in his car and then I would have known if he was going to stop by the diner or not. I cursed my haste and stupidity. I'll organise myself better next time, I vowed.

Over the next few days, I had a lot of time to think about my plan of action. In fact, I had the house to myself for the most part as Declan, Lucy and Bernadette were going to two different GAA Christmas parties and would be out pretty much all day for two days in a row. I told Declan I wouldn't be up to it, what with still being on the painkillers for my arm, and for once, he didn't try to change my mind. He seemed content that he'd found a replacement for me in Bernadette.

I spent time pondering on a less time-consuming method to achieve my goal of bumping into Seán. I know I could have been doing other things with all this time on my hands, but I couldn't focus on anything else. Seán lived in my brain now and he became my mission.

I would forget about the possibility of a lunchtime meeting. After all, he would only have five minutes to spare on his lunch break and that wouldn't be a satisfactory amount of time to spend with him. I would need to catch him leaving the clinic and either corner him there and then, or follow him to check if he goes into the diner. That would be the ideal situation, if I happened to walk into the diner and find him there already eating alone. Then again, if I followed him and he didn't pull into the diner, I would be on foot, so wouldn't be able to mark his trail further afield. Best to nab him, if possible, outside the clinic and invite him to eat with me.

On Friday, I arranged for Bernadette to take Lucy again for the afternoon and told her Declan would collect her after work. I felt a little bad asking Bernadette, when I saw how tired she still looked after all the recent GAA partying. Oh well, I concluded, all self-inflicted and a woman of her age should know better.

I groomed myself immaculately in anticipation of my 'chance' meeting with Seán. I blow-dried my long, dark hair and curled the ends at the front. I applied heavy makeup to conceal any remaining remnants of bruises and scars. I wore dark eye-shadow to achieve the smoky eye effect. I had only learned how to do this recently from the waiting room magazines and YouTube clips. I thought it suited me, especially with my hair down, and figure-hugging clothing. I chose a deep purple silk blouse that hung on my frame and tucked it into a tight black skirt with black tights and high heels.

I took a step back from the mirror and found that I was more than satisfied with my new look. I looked like a modern, vampish socialite, bang on trend. Why didn't I ever focus on my appearance before now, I wondered. I guess I never invested enough time in myself. I had gathered from my vast self-help reading that it's true what they say— life really does begin at forty!

I got plenty of admiring glances on the bus on the way in. Even the bus driver tried to chat me up.

'Christmas party night, is it?' he asked with a wink.

'Yes!' I smiled back. 'I can't wait!'

It was four-thirty when I arrived at the clinic car park. I spotted Seán's car, although I wasn't a hundred percent sure. It was dark when we left the diner at our last meeting, but I was pretty certain his was a black Volkswagen Golf. It was freezing out, so I took shelter in the bookshop, which would be open until six o'clock. Surely, he would come out by then. I really didn't want to loiter around the car park on a cold, dark evening.

Initially, I received friendly glances from the shop assistants, but after forty-five minutes hovering by the window pretending to browse, one or two of them approached me and asked if I needed any help or whether I was intending to buy. I assured them that I just couldn't make up my mind. I was starting to panic internally that maybe Seán wasn't working today. Could he be sick? I recognised two other staff members leaving the clinic, but no sign of him.

An hour passed and I was beginning to feel both uncomfortable and unwanted in the book shop. It dawned on me that the staff seemed eager to close up shop as soon as possible, what with it being a cold, dark evening so close to Christmas. I supposed they all wanted to get home or go out for Christmas drinks. It was obvious I was in the way. I finally chose a book called *How To Leave Your Husband Without Scarring Your Children For Life*. It was five-forty-five now and the shutters were half down—*talk about a hint!* I approached the till to pay. The only problem was the till wasn't near the window, so I lost sight of the car park for roughly two minutes.

I almost tripped in my high heels trying to get out of the shop to search for Seán's car and ensure I hadn't missed him. My eyes popped in disbelief, as I watched his car driving out of the car park. I sank helplessly to my knees on the pavement, heartbroken that he could have left the clinic at the exact time I was paying for this stupid book that I didn't even want!

The shop assistants rushed out to my aid, thinking I had tripped. I allowed them to help me up, admonishing myself that now I wouldn't be able to shop there anymore. They must think I'm deranged. *Damn it!*

I thanked them bashfully and got to my feet. I knew I had one last-ditch attempt for a chance encounter. Would he be starving enough to stop by the diner on his way home? It was just about six o'clock—dinner time!

I began walking down the road towards the diner. The cold air quickened my step, which seemed to grow from a brisk stride into a determined march. I searched the diner car park. It was pretty full, making it difficult to know if his car had pulled in. The lights were on inside and the open sign was flashing, so it was now or never. My hasty march transformed into a sexy strut. I flung open the doors and surveyed the interior of the diner, my goal at the forefront of my mind.

Bingo! I spotted him seated with his back to me. How would I play it? I knew I was a good actress when improvising on the spot, so I didn't make a plan. I simply walked over.

'Oh Seán, Seán, is that you?'

He got a fright and looked up with bloodshot, weary eyes.

'Oh! Hi, Mrs Caw ... Cara, hi, how are you?'

'Oh you know, I'm still in recovery. And how are you? You look ... tired.' The poor petal, I thought.

'Do I? Oh yeah, it was the last clinic before

Christmas and everyone wants to be well, so, you know, they're coming in now for anything and everything. A lot of minor complaints actually, but that's always the way at this time of year.'

I pulled out the chair opposite him and sat down, without waiting for an invitation. I didn't have time for formalities and anyway, I figured it was a perfectly reasonable thing to do.

Chapter Thirteen

'YOU DON'T MIND, do you?' But before he had a chance to answer, I beckoned over the waiter.

'I'll have what he's having!' I beamed.

'Cara, you really don't need to join me. I'm exhausted after a long, arduous day. I'm afraid I won't be good company. Don't you, don't you have someone to meet? You look dressed up.'

'Oh thanks, Seán, thanks for noticing! I've been working on a new look for the past few weeks. I'm glad you approve, hahaha!'

'I didn't mean to pass comments either way. I mean, it's none of my business.'

'Too late! I've already accepted your words as a compliment! Hahaahahah!'

He looked both uncomfortable and agitated. I took off my coat and revealed my cast.

'How is your arm, Mrs Cawley?'

'We're on first-name terms Seán, remember?'

'Yes, it's just that it's been a while and I'm very tired.'

'My arm has improved. I think I'm getting the cast off soon after Christmas! Did Linda tell you what happened? You know, when you discussed my history over the phone?'

'Em, yes, as far as I recall, she did. I'm sorry you took a turn for the worst.'

'I miss our chats, Seán. Our weekly phone consultations. They were valuable in my recovery. Just hearing your dulcet tones once a week and heeding your well-informed advice. It made such a difference to my mood. Is there any way we could resume some sort of contact again?'

'Oh well, Linda is your GP now. She will …'

'Look, Linda is fine. She's dotting the i's and crossing the t's. She's doing her job, but I need more.'

We were interrupted by the arrival of the burgers. We thanked the waiter and I continued.

'I need more input from my GP, you know what I mean?'

'Em, no actually, I don't.'

'I need a more holistic approach, shall we say.'

He sighed, exasperated, and looked down at his burger.

'Let's eat, you look starving!' I decided.

'Yes, I need to … yes, thanks.'

He devoured his burger and I nibbled at mine, as I was too busy watching him opening his mouth to take every bite. Luckily, he was so focussed on consuming his food that he didn't clock me observing him, or at least, he chose not to notice. When he finished he tried to make excuses that he had to get home.

'But why? Don't you want dessert? You said you were hungry.'

'To be honest, Mrs Cawley, as a doctor, I really shouldn't be seen socialising with one of my patients.'

'Ex-patients!' I retorted.

'Yeah, even still, I should go.'

'Oh? Have you any plans?'

'Yes, yes I do.'

I stood up to walk out with him and followed him to the till. He paid for his burger and turned to walk out. I threw money at the cashier and almost fell over trying to catch up with Seán.

'Where are you off to? I have Christmas drinks plans myself. That's why I ... I made the effort tonight.'

'I'm going to a gig in *Trailers*. They've a good band tonight. Enjoy your Christmas drinks, Mrs Cawley.' And just like that, he was gone.

'Cara!' I shouted after him. Then, faded to a whisper. 'Cara, not Mrs Cawley, remember?'

Oh no! That's not how I planned this at all! He's supposed to be swooning all over me now! I don't care if he's tired! This was all wrong. How could he not match my eagerness? Was he just trying to be professional? I was so close. There was no way I was giving up now.

I was freezing, standing in the car park watching his car pull away. I walked across the road into a pub for some warmth. I ordered a hot whiskey and perched myself on a stool by the bar to plan my next move. I actually only ever had a hot whiskey at Christmas time before falling into bed, but I badly needed warming up and thought this would do the trick.

I Googled *Trailers* and found out that the gig would start at nine o'clock. Damn! I cursed to myself that it was only 7.20 now. I had no intention of actually going to the gig. It would be too loud and crowded, and totally not my scene. But I simply had to see Seán again tonight. I saw on the map that Trailers was very near a cinema. I checked the movies later.

There was one starting at 8.45pm—an epic war movie. Shucks, I thought, but the timing would be perfect. It would end around the same time as the gig would finish. It would take me a half-hour to get there by bus. I could head into the movie around 8.30, so I'd just about had time to finish my drink. No hanging around outside in the cold. I didn't know, but I sincerely hoped Seán was a drinker. Some alcohol combined with his tiredness should make him more amenable than he was in the diner. I congratulated myself on hatching a plan of action like this off the cuff. I was getting good at this.

✧   ✧   ✧

I RANG DECLAN and explained I was meeting an old friend, Beatrice.

'Yes, we've just had dinner and now we're thinking of going into the town centre to catch a movie and maybe a drink after.'

He informed me Lucy was in bed and started telling me who tomorrow's match was against, but I cut him off, saying it was loud in the restaurant and I couldn't hear him very well.

I read the first chapter of my book and realised it wasn't as bad as the extremely long-winded, un-catchy title. I stuffed it back in my bag, finished my drink and went to catch the bus.

I spotted Trailers two doors down from the cinema. It was actually opposite my bus stop for home and there was a taxi rank nearby, so it would be feasible to concoct a good excuse about why I was hanging around the vicinity.

The movie was epically long, harrowing and heroic at the same time. I enjoyed it on the whole, despite leaving for twenty minutes and reading my book on the toilet halfway through, at the boring middle bit. I reckoned I caught up on what had likely happened and appreciated the war story overall. It was just about a quarter past eleven when it ended. I went to the cinema bathroom to touch up my hair and makeup before darting outside to search the street for Seán. There were crowds of people drifting in and out of pubs along the way. It must definitely have been the place to be in Dublin on the Friday night before Christmas. Everyone seemed young and attractive and fashionable. I felt so far removed from the social scene, that I'd forgotten it existed.

I got many admiring glances from men young enough to be my son, but I just looked the other way and tried my best to ignore any advances. I searched the streets and stood where people were exiting after the gig. I approached a girl on her way out and asked if the gig was over. She said it was, but the pub was still full, as people were getting their last orders in.

I tried to walk in against the line of traffic on their way out, but the bouncer stopped me and told me they were closing and not serving any-more. I insisted I didn't want a drink and was only looking for a friend. I must have looked respecta-ble or honest or both, as he conceded and let me through.

It was hot, sweaty and still crowded, despite the fact that dozens of people had just left. I lurked by the wall or in the corners and scanned the floor. It was mainly groups of guys huddled together laughing over pints. I noticed very few couples and very few females. I thought for a moment that I spied Jim's wife, Claire, on her way out with friends, but then realised it couldn't have been her. Sure, what would she be doing out this late in a grungy bar on a Friday night? I mean, at her age and everything.

I had forgotten to check the name of the band who had been playing, but the posters dotted around told me it could have been a singer songwriter, called Anita, or else a band, with a devilishly handsome looking frontman, called Jack. I could see why he'd attract a crowd. I searched with my eagle eye, but couldn't see Seán anywhere. I moved further afield, against the flow of people on their way out.

'Hi gorgeous!' One guy smiled at me. They were a very friendly bunch indeed. I realised my age wouldn't be an impediment if I wanted to meet someone tonight. All these young guys were turning a blind eye to the fact that I was old enough to be their mother, or else with my vampish dark makeup, it was possible that I looked considerably younger. I wasn't sure, but felt confident nonetheless that the effort I'd gone to was worth it. At that point, the barman caught my eye and beckoned me over.

'I have this poured,' he said, 'but the buyer just left. It's Cab Sav. Do you want it? On the house, obviously.'

'Oh, I told the bouncer I wasn't drinking. I'm just, em, looking for someone.'

'Hey, no worries, I won't tell on you! You may as well enjoy a glass while you're looking.' With that, he moved on, busying himself with clearing the rest of the glasses from the bar. It had been ages since I'd had a glass of wine, but wow, it tasted good. I felt the warm liquid travel down my throat and into my stomach, leaving a trail of delicious toxins darting straight to my brain. Oooh, this felt so yummy, but I mustn't let it distract me from my mission.

Bingo! I mouthed to myself for the second time that night. I spotted him huddled in a group of three well-built, good-looking young men. Even his friends were equally as delicious as him, I beamed. Just the sight of him overpowered me completely. I enjoyed watching him, unnoticed. I could have stayed there all night admiring his chiselled features, messy hair and perfect eyebrows, but time was not on my side. He only had half a pint left, so I knocked back my beverage and slipped on outside the club to 'stage' where I would surprisingly and coincidentally bump into him at this ungodly hour on a Friday night.

Twenty minutes later he came out, still laughing. All three of them were talking very loudly and animatedly, and quite probably drunkenly too. As they walked out, I noticed him stumble a little. *Yes! He's hammered. Poor petal couldn't handle those pints, what with being so tired after a busy week at work. He needs someone like me to look after him.* They were approaching the long queue at the taxi rank. Perfect! Here's my opportunity, I thought.

I followed them and joined the line. For a second, I hesitated when a voice pleaded between my ears—'*What in God's name are you doing?*' Whose voice was it? Declan's? The voice of reason? My conscience? I didn't know, but I chose to ignore it, spurred on by the alcohol I'd recently consumed. I reached out my hand, my ringless, functioning left hand, and touched his back.

'Seán, Seán is that you? What a coincidence bumping into you again like this!'

He turned around, looking worse for wear.

'Eh, hi, what are you doing here?'

'Oh, remember I told you I was going for Christmas drinks? We were over there in Chaplains and I missed my last bus, so ....'

'Oh, did you have a good night?' Seán tried to be polite, as his friends looked on.

'Yes, did you?'

'Yeah, thanks.'

'Actually, I wanted to talk to you in private.' His friends raised their eyes, smiled and turned away. I reached out and gently directed him towards the wall and out of the queue. He pointed towards his friends helplessly, but they shooed him off saying they'd call him when they moved up the line a little.

I had him now, just where I wanted him. I felt like Walter White. I was Walter White! I had the power, not exactly the ammunition that Walt would have had, but I had something better. I had feminine intuition, interwoven with a little whiskey and wine. I knew exactly what was best for this young man before me and I was in control.

'Seán, you look tired. I'm worried about you.' I realised I still had my hand on his arm from when I led him from the queue, but it seemed like he didn't notice. The few units of alcohol allowed me to lose my inhibitions and gave me the Dutch courage I needed, so I left my hand where it was, touching him.

He laughed a little at my concern before replying. 'I told you, work is crazy right now. I know I must seem a bit of a mess, but, em ...'

I moved my hand up to his face and crept closer to him. He reached for my hand to remove it, but I wouldn't let him. I whispered in his ear. 'Look at your beautiful face. You work too hard.' He was unaware of his friends looking on, as we whispered to each other, but I overheard one of them. 'Well, he's pulled! Better not disturb him.' And with that, they moved towards the top of the taxi line.

Seán stood there slouching against the wall, drunk and vulnerable, staring into my dark, smoky eyes. 'Cara.' He looked down in efforts to avoid my intense stare. 'Happy Christmas, okay? I gotta go.'

'Wait, just a minute. It's Friday night. You've no work tomorrow. Just wait a minute.'

I stroked his face and pushed my hand around the side of his head, massaging his scalp. He closed his eyes and groaned a little. 'I shouldn't ... We shouldn't ...'

'Shush.' I leaned in and enveloped his mouth in mine. We kissed. Bingo! Mission accomplished! I screamed in my mind. He tasted and smelled of beer. I would never let Declan near me after a night in the pub, but then Declan didn't look like Seán.

Seán's friends laughed and muttered something about him being a fast mover and I caught them with the corner of my eye getting into a taxi, content that their mate would be well looked after.

Seán hesitated initially. Of course he did, he was young and intoxicated and didn't know what he wanted. But I knew. I knew not just what he wanted, but also what he needed. And he needed me to take charge and look after him in a way that only I could. It seemed my sheer intent persuaded him to concede, and he leaned towards me. My one active arm was busy caressing, massaging and squeezing his face, scalp and ear, in that order. I delighted in eliciting yearning, surrendering groans from him. I felt more powerful than I'd ever felt in my whole life.

'Take me home with you, Seán.'

In his inebriated state, he paused and looked at me. Like, he really studied me, before offering himself to be led. It was a good decision. Perfectly reasonable in fact, although I was sure I heard him belch on the way to the taxi queue.

Chapter Fourteen

WE SCOOCHED INTO the backseat of the taxi as if we were boyfriend and girlfriend. I was on top of the world. My fantasy was in motion. It was happening. Really happening. This was the beginning of the rest of my life. A new life. Just me, Seán and Lucy, of course. The three of us, just the three of us.

'Seán, what's your address? We can't go to my place tonight, okay?'

'Oh, eh, yeah it's ... em...'

All of a sudden, he blinked rapidly and looked at me again, as if he was only now realising who I was.

'Cara, Mrs Cawley, listen, we can't do this, we...'

I knew I had to act quickly, so I moved closer to him to silence his protests. He turned away, but I reached for his head and turned it towards me, so I could lean in and kiss him again.

'No,' he said and turned his head, this time pushing my hand away. I got a fright and bumped my left arm off the door.

'Ow!' I bellowed. 'My arm!'

That's when the taxi driver intervened.

'Is everything okay back there?'

There was no reply.

'Hey! Is the lady okay?'

'Yes, she is,' Seán replied, obviously pissed off.

I realised then that I'd lost him and the pain of that was worse than the shooting darts up my arm.

Seán turned away from me and never turned back. He gave the taxi driver his address and silence ensued. It seemed as if he couldn't bear to look at me. He must have felt my hand touching his leg and he surely heard me whimpering. 'I'm okay, love, really, I'm okay.' But he turned his head and ignored me. I was clutching at straws at this stage. I called his name softly and squeezed his knee, but he didn't budge or look my way. I knew there was no point anymore, especially when he gave directions for a shortcut to the taxi driver. He searched his wallet and threw a twenty at him as soon as the car stopped. He almost fell out the door. I really didn't think he was THAT drunk, but maybe I hadn't been paying enough attention to him.

The taxi driver checked his phone and stopped for long enough for me to watch Seán stumble and mutter expletives on his way to his apartment. I rolled down the window and called him again, in case he changed his mind, but got no response and then the taxi moved off.

'Are you alright, miss?'

I nearly bit the driver's head off when I snapped back. 'Yes, yes, I am.' Bitterness began to seep into my veins on the rest of the journey home.

That cold, venomous bastard! How dare he turn away from me! And all the trouble I went to for him tonight! That's nearly a whole Friday that I'll never get back! Not to mention the weeks of copious planning that went into orchestrating our encounter tonight. Does he think I've nothing better to do? Who does he think he is, rejecting me like that?

I was seething now and barked once more at the driver. 'Actually, no! No! I'm not okay! That drunken, nasty piece of work just ruined my life, okay?'

'But your arm, did he hurt your arm?'

'Yes, my arm, and every other part of me.' My voice wavered and I sat back, exhausted. I thought of every expletive I'd ever heard and called Seán each and every one of them. I didn't utter any of them aloud of course, but the mere act of cursing someone in my head took it out of me. I wasn't used to bad language, but boy, did it feel good right now to unleash everything, even if it was just internally, for my ears only.

I paid the balance and the driver handed me his

card.

'Look, I don't like what I think went on back there. I'm sick of posh boys having their way with young ladies in the backseat. I've been driving this taxi for nearly thirty years now and I'll tell you one thing—there's no such thing as a gentleman in Dublin anymore. These young fellas just want one thing and if they can't get it, they turn on anyone and anything. You wouldn't believe the things I've seen in this taxi over the years. Look, what I'm saying is, if you need a witness, call me, okay? I'm so sick of this crap every weekend, y'know what I mean? And one more thing, don't go out with HIM again!'

I dismissed the driver's comments, but took the card nonetheless. I sneaked in quietly and couldn't face removing my makeup. I was so weary and pale now that I looked like I was in a Halloween costume. My eye makeup had smudged from rubbing my eyes, but I didn't care. I would change the pillow case in the morning.

Declan was fast asleep on his side of the bed. He always slept so close to the edge that I often wondered how he managed not to fall out. I lay awake in angst for an hour, going back over the events of the night. I tried every meditative practice I could remember, before giving up and turning over. When I stopped trying to fall asleep, I fell asleep. I fell into such a deep sleep that I didn't hear Declan getting Lucy up and leaving the house at ten o'clock in the morning.

When I finally awoke, I felt leaden. An immense weight crushed against my head and I rolled over, not wanting to get up and face the day ahead. I refused to check the time in case it was morning, but the light bore through the duvet and pierced my eyelids. I forced myself to roll over and almost cried when I saw that it was after eleven am. I wondered where the hell Declan and Lucy were.

I found a note on the kitchen table, saying they'd gone to the zoo, as Bernadette had won free tickets at bingo. Then, they planned to go to a Gaelic match and they'd probably get dinner at the club. A family day out, I thought, sarcastically.

I made coffee and convinced myself to eat something, all the while wishing I had some benzos left to get me through the day. I would have loved a magic sleeping pill to send me into the land of dreams, but maybe I was better off without them, as the only person I'd ever dreamt about was Seán.

Seán, Seán ... I wondered how much he remembered from last night? I thought about the passionate kiss we shared and still felt the touch of his face, hair and neck on the palms of my hands. The softness of his skin, the hardness of his chest and the desire in his eyes. He was into me, I could tell. He reciprocated gladly until something made him change his mind in the taxi. What was it? What made him reject me so vehemently? I was sure he didn't have a girlfriend and his mates seemed to be egging him on. What was his problem? I didn't like the mystery of it all. I couldn't get my head around why he would reject me like that all of a sudden.

I showered lethargically and dressed in jeans, runners and the baggiest jumper I could find. I put on a face mask to heal the dehydrated, clogged skin on my cheeks and temple. And then I sat down on the couch with some toast and read the rest of that awful book I'd bought with the long-winded title—*How To Leave Your Husband Without Scarring Your Children For Life*. In hindsight, there were actually a few useful titbits in it, so I satisfied myself that it wasn't a complete waste of money.

I Googled Seán Dempsey to see what would come up. I found his glorious image twice and links to his Facebook and Instagram. I considered signing up for both to get more info on him and his likes, but the whole world of social media frightened me senseless. I had avoided it thus far and the fear of having only a handful of people I could refer to as 'friends' put me off. I'd rather avoid the embarrassment of having only five friends following me, when I knew most others had hundreds.

Declan had a family Facebook page anyway, and he shared updates of Lucy's progress regularly. His friends were mainly club members, workmates and extended family. He posted cute baby pictures of Lucy, first day at school and plenty of pictures of her running around the pitch with other kids, kicking a football. I featured in one or two of his updates and got lots of sympathetic messages and get well wishes when he posted a close-up of my broken arm in a cast. It all meant very little to me, though. I wasn't interested in what was going on in other people's lives, but still feigned the odd 'Oooh' and 'Ahhh' when he showed me photos of the latest new baby or wedding or club members glammed up for a dinner dance.

It was almost six o'clock and I half expected them to burst through the door at any second, but they didn't. I got stuck into some neglected housework to pass the time. I really had let things go recently, what with being one armed. To give Declan his due, he had kept up with the hoovering and carried the heavy baskets of laundry downstairs for me. Things like dusting and cleaning bathrooms had been overlooked though, so I caught up with that as best I could with my good hand.

Eight o'clock came and went with no sign of them still. It was Lucy's bedtime. I wondered if maybe they were in Bernadette's having a plate of sausages, as has often been the case lately. I decided to go and collect Lucy myself. Sure, Declan rarely checked his phone and they were only next door.

I pressed the doorbell numerous times, but got no answer. I realised it must be broken, so I walked around to the side entrance. There was no doorbell, but I tried the handle and discovered it was unlocked. I opened it gently to check for signs of life. I heard noise in the living room. They were probably watching TV, so I made my way inside. Nothing could have prepared me for the horrific sight that confronted me!

Bernadette was sprawled out on the couch with her skirt pulled up to her thighs and Declan was rubbing oil upwards on her legs, quite far north, as far as I could make out. I almost retched at the vision.

'Ewwww, what are you doing, Declan?' I roared.

The two of them jumped in fright at the sound of my voice and Bernadette rolled off the couch, in efforts to see who was standing at the door.

'Jesus, Cara, look what you've done!' Declan piped up when he realised Bernadette had fallen with a bang.

'Ahh, me shoulder, ahhh!' she screamed.

I was left speechless, apart from a tiny whisper. 'Where's Lucy?'

'Bernie, Bernie, are you okay?' Declan leapt to her side.

'Oh, me shoulder, me shoulder, ahhhh!!' Bernadette was crying.

Declan looked up. 'She's asleep in the front room. Will you take her home to bed? I'm gonna bring Bernie to the hospital.'

'I can't carry Lucy with one arm. You'll have to carry her in, Declan. And ... *"Bernie, Bernie?"* Like, what the hell?'

'Ah, for Christ's sake, Cara. Bernie, Bernadette, you know who I mean!'

'Ahhhhh, me shoulder Declan, is it broken?'

'I don't know, Bernadette, can you move it?'

'Ahhhh!'

'Jayziz, I better call an ambulance. If it's broken, I can't move you, y'know. I may only make it worse. What do you think, Cara?'

'What do I think? WHAT DO I THINK? I haven't an effing clue, Declan, but I want you to carry Lucy into her bed NOW!'

'Go on, Declan, you better do as she says,' Bernadette struggled through her obvious pain.

'Bernie, I can't leave you alone like this on the floor! Cara, you wait with her. I'll call the ambulance and bring Lucy to bed. You got that, Cara?'

'Ahhhhh!' howled Bernie.

'Yes, yes, now get Lucy, so I can go home too!'

Declan proceeded to dial for an ambulance. As

soon as he got through and arranged it, he picked up Lucy, who had slept through all the chaos, and carried her into our house to tuck her up in bed. Meanwhile, I tended to Bernadette's requests.

'A clean nightie, Cara, from the top drawer and the dressing gown hanging at the back of the bedroom door. Ooooohhhh! Aaaahhhhh! And you know yourself, Cara, a change of undies and my, ahhhh, toothbrush. Good girl, thanks love. Aaahhhhhh, the bloody pain!'

When Declan arrived back with his backpack in tow, I met him in the hall.

'What's that?' I hissed.

'It's an overnight bag. I reckon it could be a long wait in A&E, considering how long we waited recently with your arm,' he answered innocently with a face full of concern.

I registered his concern and I raised my alarm. 'Declan, what the HELL was going on with you and Bernadette on the couch? Are you having some kind of sordid, kinky affair? She's old enough to be your mother!'

He gestured with his hands, like a politician defending his position. 'Look Cara, there's an emergency. I'm not getting into this now, okay? I'll go in the ambulance with Bernie ... Bernadette. She'll need some support. You go back inside to Lucy.'

My alarm turned into a blasting siren at this

point. 'You're planning to go with her? Once she's in the ambulance, they'll look after her. She doesn't need you! And what about work in the morning? You'll be in the hospital all night!'

'Cara, as if you give a shit about my work! You're just being selfish now. Bernadette might have a broken shoulder because of YOU. She's our neighbour and good friend, not to mention Lucy's childminder and she's in there on the floor, crying out in pain. It's perfectly reasonable that I accompany her to the hospital, right?'

Chapter Fifteen

I HEARD VIA text from Declan that Bernadette's shoulder was indeed broken. I was raging that our new childminder was out of action so soon, but grateful I would be getting my own cast off within the week. I would take full charge of Lucy now that Bernadette was incapacitated. I had a sneaky feeling that the old dear had an ulterior motive with all her offers of help to mind Lucy. The auld floozy, I thought, she just wanted to get her hands on Declan the whole time!

And what was that kinky interaction I'd witnessed last night? My husband nuzzling the groin of a granny! I was sure Bernadette was the same age as Declan's mother—seventy-five. How could Declan find an OAP like her in any way attractive?

Then, I thought about who I found attractive—Seán. How could he? How dare he have the nerve to reject me like that! Maybe I should have gone for one of his friends instead. That would have served him right! Next time I'd make a beeline for the tall, dark guy. He looked like a doctor too and much less drunk than Seán. Why didn't I think of that last Friday! *I'm no Walter White. I'm just not cunning enough, not yet, but I'm learning. Next time, I'll make him green with envy when he sees me all over his more mature, better-looking best friend.*

I put Lucy to bed, half-heartedly going through the motions of reading her a bedtime story. She seemed more than content anyway, and I had other things on my mind.

The following morning, I received a second text from Declan saying he had left the hospital at 11am and gone into work from there. He planned to return to Bernadette's bedside afterwards and wouldn't be home until late. I supposed I'd have to wait until then to have it out with him.

Tuesday morning came around again and it was time for my appointment with Doctor Linda. It was the first time I walked confidently and unselfconsciously into the office. I had an inner epiphany—it's happening, I thought. What they say in all the midlife crises books I've read is true—forty-year-olds literally don't give a monkeys about what anyone thinks of them! It was happening to me a couple of months shy of turning forty, but I couldn't find any other explanation as to why I felt so diva-like, blazing through the office. I held my head high and beamed outwardly at everyone.

Linda was waiting for me.

'Good morning, Cara! You look vibrant today!

How are you?'

'Morning! I feel physically well. I've no pain in my arm and I'm only dying to get the cast off. But mentally, I'm not so strong.'

'Why so?'

'Well, I just found out my husband is having an affair with our next door neighbour, who also happens to be our childminder!'

'Oh my goodness! That's horrific!'

'Yes, yes it is. It's very raw. I haven't really processed it yet.'

'I see here in my records that Doctor Seán mentioned you were going through a separation a few months ago.'

'Oh, did he now? Did he say that? In his dreams I am!' I could use this to my advantage. I wasn't going to let Seán ruin any more of my life.

'Cara! What on earth do you mean?'

'Well, I'm sure he'd love to believe I'm single! HE would!'

'Why?'

'Look, to tell you the truth, he's another reason why my mental health isn't what it should be. I'm stressed.'

Linda raised her eyebrows questioningly. I carried on.

'He is stressing me out if you must know.'

'But Cara, you're not his patient any more.'

'No, but ...' Thoughts raced through my mind.

He rejected me. This is all his fault. He shouldn't have let me imagine us together. He shouldn't have led me on. This is all on him.

'What?' Linda beckoned.

'That doesn't preclude me from seeing him.'

'When did you see him?'

'Friday night.'

'Night? So, it wasn't during surgery hours?'

'No.'

'Well, it's possibly none of my business then,' Linda said, trying as ever to be professional.

'You think?'

'Doctor Dempsey is an esteemed colleague of mine and I don't feel comfortable discussing his out-of-hours contact with you.'

'Even if that's the very reason I'm having thoughts about self-harming again?'

'Are you?'

'Yes.'

'Very well then. We should discuss it. Why are you having these thoughts?'

'Mainly because I've been … I've been assault-ed. No, I mean, wounded, by Doctor Seán!'

'Cara, please! What on earth do you mean?'

'He … he hurt me on Friday night,' I said with a sob. I took a packet of tissues out of my hand-bag.

'This is a very serious accusation, Cara. Do you understand?'

'Yes.' He deserves this, I told myself. He shouldn't have pushed me away in the taxi. It's time now. Time for me to get my revenge. I was still seething after the events of that night. All those feelings of disappointment and dejection bubbled up right there and then in Linda's clinic.

'Okay, tell me what happened.'

'I went out with friends on Friday night to catch a movie and Christmas drinks. Later, when I got to the line for a taxi home, Seán and his mates happened to be in front of me in the queue.'

'Okay, so it was a chance meeting. Go on.'

'I, I mean we ... said hello to each other. He seemed highly intoxicated. I know that because I don't really drink that much, so I remember everything.'

I wiped a tear from my eye before continuing. The little tear surprised me, but it came at the right moment. Packed a punch and added some impact, in my humble opinion.

'Yes, well em, he was very happy to see me and his friends egged him on quite a bit. He ... he took my arm, you know, my one good arm, and led me over to the wall, away from the taxi queue.'

'Wait, what about his friends? What did they do?'

'Oh, they saw. They saw everything, believe me! They just thought *"Seánie"* was getting some action and they encouraged him to no end.'

'Oh, I'm very surprised by that. I know some of Doctor Seán's friends and they're very respected, experienced GPs. I couldn't imagine them displaying such laddish behaviour, but I suppose I don't exactly know which guys were out with him that night.'

'Who do you know?'

'James, I was thinking of James.'

'No, the one I have in mind, I don't think his name was James.' I had no idea.

'Ok, carry on anyway.'

'He was very touchy-feely and basically tried to kiss me. I had no choice in the matter! I thought he wanted to talk, you know? He seems like a nice young man. I thought he only wanted to talk, but his words were slurred, his eyes half closed and he launched himself at me. There was no way I could escape him.'

'And where were his friends at this stage?'

'Gone … gone in a taxi.'

'Did anyone try to rescue you?'

'Midnight on a Friday night in Dublin, you know, nobody even knows what their own name is by then. No, nobody approached me.'

'So, he kissed you? Is that what you're implying? Without your consent, I mean.'

'Yes, I had no say in the matter. I was actually concerned about him, because he was in such a state. Foolish, I know…'

'No, not at all. He's a young guy, drunk in Dublin. His friends left him alone. You're a mother, I totally understand why you would be concerned about him.'

'Oh, oh thanks, Linda, yes of course. You're a mother yourself? Aren't you?'

'Yes, my baby boy is nearly one,' she smiled, before continuing. 'So, how did you get away from him?'

'Well, that's where all my anxiety stems from. You see, after I pulled away from him, he tried to pull me back. He told me not to worry, everything would be okay if I just listened to him. He assured me he was my GP after all, and I guess, I don't know, I guess that made me trust him... Again, I know, foolish of me...'

'No, Cara, not at all. I see where you're coming from.'

'He told me he'd had enough and wanted to go home. He noticed his friends had left him, and asked me to share a taxi with him. I looked around and had no other options either, as my friends had also gone, so I said yes. I ... I ... sorry,' I wiped more tears from my mascara'd face. 'Sorry, I got into the taxi with him and, oh, how I regret that decision now. He was inebriated and pulled me towards him. I remember shouting something like, "*Sean! I thought you just wanted to go home! What are you doing?*" But he grabbed me. He, em, he hurt me, really hurt me, you know, my arm in the cast. I screamed, but he didn't seem to care. He just wanted what he wanted.'

'Did the taxi driver intervene when you screamed?'

'Well, he was very concerned about me. He gave me his card afterwards, in case I ever needed a witness, you know, if I wanted to take things further.'

'Okay, okay, Cara, here, have a sip of water. Are you well enough to continue?'

'Yes. He wanted me to go home with him, but I refused. I told him I was married, I mean, look at my wedding ring. How could he have doubted it?'

'Yes, I see your ring. In fact, I've never seen you without it. And you certainly never mentioned a separation to me. That's why I ... I suppose I questioned Seán's analysis of the situation.'

'Did you?' But then she changed the subject.

'When you refused him, what happened next?'

'He sort of hit out and caught my arm. You know, I got such a shock. He struck me, whether he meant to or not. My doctor, who I trusted above and beyond anyone else, hurt me! Linda, can you believe he would do such a thing?'

'Cara, Cara, of course I believe you! How did you get away from him, especially if you were stuck in the taxi with him?'

'It was very late and I was tired. I just wanted

to get home to my husband and daughter.'

'Of course, of course you did.'

'He was angry that I refused him, very angry, but I was adamant. I just wanted to get home. He threw some money at the taxi driver and almost fell out of the taxi and slammed the door so hard, it made me jump. I was already in pain from him hitting out at me, and this gave me another jolt. But I was relieved. I mean, if he didn't get out of the taxi, I just can't bear to think what might have happened!'

'I take it you got home safely?'

'Yes, yes, I did, in floods of tears of course, but my husband and child were fast asleep and I, oh you know yourself being a mom, I didn't have the heart to wake them up. So I put on a brave face and went to bed, telling myself I would deal with it all the next day. I fell into such a deep sleep that I slept in very late and when I woke up, they were gone for the day. So I wallowed in self-pity, waiting to talk to a professional such as yourself about my terrifying ordeal.'

'And did you discuss it with your husband when he got home that evening?'

'He didn't get home until late. I ... I didn't know it then ... he went to collect Lucy at the childminder's and stayed there for a very long time. She just lives next door to us, so I eventually went in myself to get Lucy. It was way past her bedtime. Of course, now I know the reason for all the unexplained late nights. He wasn't working late at all!' I paused here, wide-eyed, for impact.

'I … I caught them in the act on the couch and the worst thing of all was Lucy was in the house, being minded. She was asleep in the next room, but Lord, how could someone do that? With their own child present while they committed adultery? It beggars belief! So, you see, Linda, I had no one to turn to, with all of this domestic chaos going on. I had no one to confide in about my … assault, until … until today. Thank God, I was due to see you today. I didn't know where else to turn.'

'Cara, with so much turmoil in your personal life right now, you did the right thing to wait for your appointment. Now, let's work out what the next step is for you. Would you like my assistance in reporting Doctor Dempsey's behaviour?'

'Oh, no, no thank you, Linda. I'm not ready to take it further yet. I'd rather discuss it with a friend first. She's a lawyer and she can advise me. You know, I need time to process everything. Could you just keep this purely confidential for the moment, until I decide what to do?'

'Of course, yes of course. You do what you have to do. Get some advice, talk it out with a trusted friend. That's perfectly reasonable, Cara.'

Chapter Sixteen

IDEAS OF REVENGE swirled around in my head as I bussed it home. I didn't have another appointment to see Linda until early in the new year, due to the Christmas break. Plenty of time for me to plan my next move.

A week after Christmas, I would be getting my cast removed and thus able to drive to my next appointment. For that reason, I decided to kick back and relax and enjoy what would probably be my last bus journey for a while. Any family outings over Christmas and Declan would drive. Declan … His image opened up in my mind. Declan. What the hell? I really hoped what I had witnessed between himself and Bernadette had been a moment of madness, due to one Guinness too many. Surely, they couldn't be … Surely, he wouldn't go there, would he?

When I actually thought about it, I realised I had absolutely no clue what turned him on. Grannies, though? In their seventies? I never would have guessed that! I assumed it would be a strong, hardy camogie player with child-bearing hips. The essence of a woman, and the polar opposite of me. But instead, he was cavorting with a senior citizen, old enough to be his mother. It really didn't bear thinking about.

No, not now, I wouldn't think about that now. I would deal with it later, when I saw Declan. I sat back and tried to appreciate the bus ride. I looked around at the other passengers, heads stuck in phones, nothing and no one remarkable. Flashbacks of Declan and Bernadette's antics refused to stop popping up in my mind, but I pushed them away, rubbing my forehead to calm the throbbing.

I peered out the window at Dublin passing. It wasn't the buildings, trees or people that struck me, but rather the movement. The movement of everyone and everything in this city just sped by the window, obstructing my focus on any one thing. It was a city on the go, showing no signs of slowing down. I compared it to my busy brain, bustling and unstoppable. I guess with a population of well over a million people, packed into a relatively small area, relentless motion was to be expected.

I got off the bus one stop early and decided to walk through the park on my way to the school to collect Lucy. Maybe the fresh air would alleviate the heaviness in my head. But I could still hear them—Declan and Bernadette. The sounds of their satisfied moans and groans lingered in my ears and contributed to my escalating headache. I carried on regardless and tried to focus on the scenery.

This was the park where I had fallen, almost two months ago. I'd been so intent on Lucy riding without her training wheels and distracted by a possible sighting of Seán, that I hadn't taken the time to observe the beauty surrounding me. It was vast, green, hilly, tree-lined and neatly paved. There were joggers, scooters and dog walkers everywhere.

A Versace baby stroller caught my eye. It was the same one I used to have for Lucy when she was a baby. I felt a pang in my chest when I got close and saw the baby in the stroller quite resembled Lucy at about six months old. It stopped me in my tracks. I froze for a minute as I watched the doting parents fuss over their new baby girl when she let out a little squeal. For a second, it reminded me of me and Declan. We were once so united just like them. I wiped away a tear and carried on for fear I'd be late for the school collection.

Lucy ran into my arms at the school gate. I shared with her the image of the baby in the park in the very same stroller that she'd had. Then, she made me promise to bring her back to the park as soon as my cast was removed, so I could push her on the swing. She broke into song after that and rattled off all the new nursery rhymes she'd learned in school.

The greenery and fresh air breathed some positivity into me, but the image of the previous evening still weighed heavily upon me. How could we carry on from here? Me, chasing a younger man with no clear signs of interest in me, and Declan, cavorting with our elderly neighbour. I mean, how could a marriage survive this?

Did I even want our marriage to survive? Did Declan? The more I thought about it, the more sentimental I became—for our relationship, our marriage and our little family. That familiar surge rose within me again, the one I'd felt in Dr Seán's waiting room. Except the last time it was a surge of feminine sensuality and empowerment. This time it felt like Mother Nature rising like a phoenix from the pit of my tummy. She sent protective, territorial waves through my bloodstream to remind me of what was mine. Or at least, what was once mine.

As I approached our driveway, I could feel tears welling up. I blinked them away and clapped for Lucy when she performed her favourite rhyme using the front door as a prop for 'One Two Buckle My Shoe'. As soon as she settled down, I decided to distract myself with housework. It was the perfect excuse to get stuff done.

✧   ✧   ✧

LATER THAT EVENING, I was wrapping Christmas gifts for Declan's mother. She'd be getting extra this year, as everything I'd bought for Bernadette was going to her now. I'd still give the Christmas tree dog biscuits to Rex, but *'Bernie'* wouldn't be getting the fleece-lined furry slippers or the bottle of whiskey. Declan's mother didn't drink, but I was sure she'd be eager to have a drop of something festive in the house for visitors. Declan shuffled in, looking exhausted.

'So, the prodigal husband returns! Doesn't Bernadette require your services this evening?'

'Ah Cara, will you play fair! The poor woman broke her shoulder.'

'Well, don't look at me as if it's my fault! What the hell were YOU doing sprawled over her half-naked body on the couch, while your daughter lay sleeping in the next room? What if Lucy woke up and caught you in the act? What then? It was a stroke of luck that it was only me who barged in!'

'A stroke of luck? You put the fear of God in Bernadette! That's why she rolled off the couch, y'know!'

'What was I supposed to do? Kneel down and massage her other leg?'

He paused and took a deep breath. 'All I'm saying, is that I think you got the wrong end of the stick.'

'Oh, does the old dear use a walking stick now,

does she?'

No response. I continued.

'Well, tell me then, what the hell was going on! Go on, here's your chance!'

'Look, Bernadette's been on her feet a lot, minding Lucy and traipsing about the GAA pitch every weekend. Her knees are in bits. She's in a lot of pain and I ... y'know, having the bit of physio experience at the club, I offered her my, em, my skills and that.'

'Why doesn't she go to a professional physio-therapist?'

'She's afraid she'll be told she needs a knee replacement and doesn't want an operation. Sure, she'd have to rest up for a couple of months, and that wouldn't suit her.' He shook his head in earnest. 'Wouldn't suit her at all. She's fierce active, she is!'

'For her age you mean, active for a senior citi-zen!'

'Active for any age, I meant.'

'Well, it didn't look like physiotherapy you were giving her. It looked more like a cheap, steamy massage in a ... in a ... I don't know, a seedy brothel!'

'Ah Cara, you're blowing things outta propor-tion now! It's just Bernadette relaxes more in the dim light and the candles. They're ... well, they're soothing, she says.'

'Does she?'

Silence.

'And what about the tights around her ankles? Is it essential to perform physio on bare legs only?'

'Well, yeah, to rub the oil in properly and penetrate the muscles …'

'Oh Lord, look, I don't want to hear any more about it. Just, stop, okay!' I couldn't. I simply had to change the subject. My headache was returning and my ears were starting to hurt. 'Now, what are we going to do after Christmas when I go back to work, Declan? Who's going to mind Lucy?'

'I don't know. Have you got a date yet?'

'No, I've an appointment on the fourth of January. I can't see myself getting another cert. My cast will be off by then. And I'm … I'm feeling stronger, I mean mentally stronger, you know.'

'Good, that's good. It means you won't need those antidepressants for much longer, will you?'

'No, I don't suppose I will. I'll see what Linda says. But what are we going to do with Lucy? Have you asked around at the club?'

'Yeah, look, we won't be stuck. There's a new creche opening up in Westin that does collections from school. Jim's wife, Claire, is a primary school teacher, as you know, and says they have places available. A lot of the school children go there. It costs a fortune and it's a bit far outta the way for us, but it would do for a month or two until we sort something out locally.'

'Yes, do it. Tell Claire to book a place for her. We have to organise something. She's back to school on the seventh of January and you never know, I could be back to work too on the same date.'

'How do you feel about that?'

'I'm ready. I'm ready to take on those bitches in the office and I won't take any more crap from them!'

'Christ, Cara! I wasn't expecting that reaction! Were they really that bad?'

'They victimised me ever since l went back after my career break. They were bitter and jealous that I got time off with Lucy and they loaded every single petty job on me, when no one else wanted it. I feel stronger now and Linda's on my side, so I won't be afraid to stand up to them. She has my back, Linda does.'

'That's great! You don't miss eh, what's his name, Seán, was it?'

'I don't want to talk about him now.'

'Oh?'

Silence ... again.

'Did you, did you fall out or something?'

'I said I don't want to talk about him, okay? Not now. So, em, how long does it take to recover from a broken shoulder? Do you think Bernadette will be able to mind Lucy again when she gets better?'

'Well, would you still want her to?'

'Yes, why not? It's so convenient with her being next door.'

'Well yeah, I just didn't think you'd want … em, under the circumstances … I don't know how long it'll take her to recover, but she seems to think she'll be in hospital for at least another month.'

'Ok, keep in touch with her. We may want her in the future as Lucy's childminder.'

'Well, she'd certainly be delighted to hear that.'

'Who's with her tonight?'

'Her sister's over from the UK for a little while.'

'Okay, visit her again as soon as the sister's gone. Bring Lucy with you. In fact, we'll all go. We'll tell her we want to go back to business as usual, once her shoulder is better. We won't be able to afford this expensive creche for more than a month or two. We still have those other loans to pay off.'

'Yeah, I know we do. I've been offered some overtime this week. Might as well do it while I can, you know, before you go back to work. I'll still be off for a few days over Christmas, of course.'

'Yes, take it when you can get it. I think I'll have an early night, Declan, okay? I'm glad we sorted things out.'

'I must say, Cara, you've been very magnanimous about the whole situation. Bernadette will be delighted there's no hard feelings.'

'Well, I wouldn't go that far. I just think we need her on board as Lucy's childminder. It's more of a business decision really. Goodnight now.'

'A business decision. Well, I won't word it quite like that to Bernie, but I see where you're coming from. Sleep well, love.'

✧　✧　✧

THE NEXT DAY, I was feeling ever so overwhelmed from recent events, so I looked for my mother's diary in an effort to ground myself. As I was leafing through her words of wisdom, I came across that taxi driver's card. The 'business decision' I spoke of with Declan the night before was still ringing in my head. Repaying those debts was a priority for us now. Everything from here on HAD to be a business decision. I decided to call him.

'Hello, my name is Cara Cawley. You gave me your card last Friday night in case I needed you as a witness. Well, I think I do.'

'Oh yes?'

'Remember that young man in the back of the taxi with me? He struck me in his drunken stupor and hurt my already broken arm. He hurt me very badly, in fact, and I think I'm going to press charges against him.'

'Ah yes, the lady with the cast on her arm. I remember now. And the posh boy. Do you need my word or something?'

'Can I count on you if he denies anything? Can you tell the guards what you saw?'

'Yes, I will, I said I would. In fact, I have a short video of him stumbling and cursing himself after he got out of my taxi. Only a few seconds. I haven't deleted it yet. I do this from time to time if there's been an incident. You see, I'm sick of these assholes getting away with murder in the back of my taxi.'

Wow! He's good. Glad I have him on my side. 'And, em, just so I know what to expect—what will you say?'

'A drunk young fella hit out at you in the backseat. You screamed and he didn't even check if you were okay. He was foul-humoured and demanded to be let out of my taxi. He stumbled into his apartment and almost fell on the ground. I saw him as I drove away. You were too upset. You were in bits.'

'Yes, yes I was. Very, very upset and I still am. Thank you for your support. That sounds like a perfectly reasonable version of events.'

Chapter Seventeen

C HRISTMAS CAME AND went with Lucy being on top of the world following the arrival of Santa Claus. Much time was spent with Declan's mother, while Bernadette remained in hospital for the Christmas period. As promised, I accompanied them to the hospital to visit her. Her face fell when she saw me walk in with them.

We let Lucy distract the proceedings with her news from school and the new friends she'd made at creche. The upbeat smile didn't leave my lips, except when I saw her shabby granny slippers pushed under the bed. I felt bad that I'd withheld the new slippers from her, deeming her an unworthy recipient of a Christmas gift in light of recent events. I'd given them to Declan's mother instead. Looks like old Bernadette could have done with them though, judging by the worn, tattered pair under the bed.

'That's lovely, Lucy dear. Cara, how are you? How's your arm?' she enquired.

'Making a full recovery now, thanks, Bernadette. I'm nearly there! And how are they treating you in hospital?' I wasn't going to give her the satisfaction of enquiring after her shoulder. We danced around the reason she was in hospital, neither of us wanting to draw attention to it.

'Oh, the nurses are lovely. They can't do enough for me and the food's not actually too bad.'

'She gets a fry up at the weekends, Cara! Isn't that a great menu?' Declan interjected. They both laughed together about their mutual love of sausages. I didn't know where to look. I was relieved when the cosy couple's sausage banter was interrupted by a nurse.

'Hi Bernie, you left this in the bathroom. Just as well you had the foresight to write your name on it, otherwise you'd never get it back. That was good thinking!' the young nurse beamed as she handed it to Bernie.

'Oh, did I? Thank you, dear,' Bernadette smiled in return.

Lucy piped up. 'Is that your toothpaste, Bernie, is it?'

'Em, yes dear, it is,' Bernie was cagey in her response.

Lucy read the label on the box, phonetically and very loudly. She sounded out each letter before blending them to make a word. 'F – i – x – o – d – e – n – t. Fixodent! Is that what it says? Am I right?'

I burst into laughter. 'It is! Well done, Lucy! All your hard work in junior infants is paying off!' Bernadette was mortified and Declan's expression was one of horror. Lucy continued. 'But that's not like our toothpaste. It's much smaller and …'

As a mother, I'm always eager to promote the education of my one and only darling child. 'You're right, Lucy. It's not toothpaste. Look what it says.' I pointed to the words and read slowly. 'Denture adhesive cream. Strong hold, seal and comfort all day long.'

Lucy looked puzzled. 'But what does that mean?'

As I said, I'm always willing to help. 'It's for very old people to stick their false teeth into their gums.'

Bernadette's head was almost under the covers now and Declan shifted uncomfortably from foot to foot as if he couldn't wait to exit. Luckily for him, the bell rang to signify that visiting time was over. As we walked to the car, I beamed. 'That was great, Declan! Highly entertaining! Tell me when you're going again and I'll join you!'

✧　✧　✧

I GOT MY cast removed as promised and my arm was back in perfect working order. I felt stronger than ever and my recent altercation with Seán in the taxi only strengthened my resolve for payback. I wouldn't let him get away with this. I'd invested so much of my thoughts and energy into our relationship, and I wasn't about to walk away now with nothing. I wanted something to show for it. I knew Walter White wouldn't stand for this mugginess and neither would I.

On January the second, I decided to carry out the first of my new year's resolutions and take the initial step of my plan of action. I channelled Barbara my boss's belligerent approach to getting what she wanted and called Seán's direct line.

'Hello.'

His voice made me melt a little, but I stood strong and ignored the flutters rising within.

'Seán, it's Cara Cawley.'

'Is it? Oh, Cara …. How are you?'

'The last time I saw you, you practically assaulted me. I just hope you're aware of that.'

'Hang on, what are you talking about?'

'You know exactly what I'm talking about and so does my solicitor.'

'What? Wait a sec, what are you alleging?'

'Alleging? I resent the use of that word! I'm not "alleging" anything! I simply relayed the facts to my solicitor and he says I have a case. Luckily, our taxi driver was paying attention to events unfolding in the backseat and he's willing to testify. You haven't a leg to stand on, I'm afraid!'

The line went dead. He hung up. I laughed at the shock of it. I was delighted with my performance! I had exceeded my own expectations this time!

✧   ✧   ✧

AN HOUR LATER, my phone rang. He must have needed time to digest that.

'Hello?'

'Hi Cara, it's Seán.'

'Oh.'

'Yeah, look, I'm sorry I hung up on you earlier. It's just the phone fell and I think I was in shock at your accusations.'

'They were allegations earlier. Now they're accusations, are they?'

'Oh, I don't want to get into that right now. I only wanted to remind you that we had a very caring doctor/patient relationship, Cara, a caring, professional one. I know you might be under pressure or struggling financially, but really, this isn't the way to improve things in your life. I know you're a perfectly reasonable person and deep down, you don't want to go through with this ... this treachery. I mean it could ruin my medical career going forward and for you, it would be a time-consuming, stressful undertaking ... Cara?

Are you still there?'

'Hmmm, so you're trying to spare me some stress, are you? My current doctor is looking after me and alleviating my stress levels far better than you ever did!'

'Look, myself and Dr Linda Craven are not in competition, you know! Your symptoms had improved when I referred you to her. But I ... I want to get back to the matter,' he pleaded.

'Well, Linda was utterly shocked to hear my version of events of that Friday night before Christmas. She couldn't believe a professional doctor would behave in such an unsavoury manner. She saw firsthand how distressed I was and asked if I needed assistance in reporting your actions to the Medical Council of Ireland. Look, Doctor Dempsey, I know you well enough at this stage. You've shown your true colours! You don't care about me! You're just trying to protect your reputation!'

'No, no, it's not like that. I care about all my patients, past and present. If you feel I led you on in some way, then I can only apologise ...'

'Led me on? Do you hear yourself? You were falling all over me that Friday night in town! You were drooling over me, until you went sour in the taxi.'

'Well, that's your version of events and I dread to think of what you told Linda. I can't even

believe you went behind my back like that. I know
I was a little intoxicated, but I definitely made the
right decision not to go home with you.'

There goes the dagger in my heart. Even now?
How could he? He didn't have to say it straight
out like that. I hated that he could still hurt me. I
hated that he still had that power over me. It only
fuelled my resolve. 'Oh, is that what you think?' I
snapped.

'Yes, of course! I'll ring Linda and set her
straight. And I'd like to speak to the taxi driver in
question please. Can you send me his details?'

'What? So you can pay him off to lie on your
behalf! No way!'

'No, I wouldn't do that. I want to hear what he
witnessed, that's all.'

'Well, I want to be present. I'll organise a meeting, but I want to make sure you don't try to sway
him from the truth.'

'Ok, I guess that's somewhat reasonable. Let
me know when and where. I'll be there.'

I SET UP the meeting at the train station, as it was
right next door to the taxi depot. Jack, the driver,
agreed to pop in at one pm on his lunch break. I
couldn't believe someone would be so kind and
give up his time just to help me, someone he barely

knew. When I thanked him over the phone, he said, 'What goes around comes around'. I made a mental note of that.

The next day, Seán arrived with an elderly couple that looked like they must be his parents. They appeared very well-to-do, like Seán, and I couldn't help but notice their looks of concern. His mother seemed stressed, as she nodded politely to me. His dad looked shattered, as if his son's predicament had kept him awake all night. I briefly thought how my dear, departed mother would feel in a situation like this, but immediately banished the thought from my head. Compassion like that would weaken my resolve and I had serious debts to pay.

I broke the ice, with noncommittal eye contact. 'This is Jack, our taxi driver. You can see here a record of his route from the night and I even kept my receipt. Would you like to ask him any questions?'

'Emmm, yes I would. Hi, Jack. Do you remember me?' Seán stepped forward.

'Yes,' Jack said and lowered his eyes in what seemed like disappointment.

'Okay, can you let us know what you remember of the taxi ride on this night? Oh, I forgot, these are my parents, George and May.'

Again Jack nodded his head in a sombre greeting, before speaking.

'I picked you up at the taxi rank. There seemed to be a lover's tiff in the backseat, but I didn't pay much attention. None of my business, but when the young lady screamed, it got my attention.'

Oh, he called me 'young'. I'm liking this guy more and more by the minute. My grimace softened momentarily.

Seán's mum looked shocked. 'Why did she scream?'

'Mom, Dad, this is utterly insane! I can assure you, it's a fabricated version of ...' The words exploded out of Seán, but Jack interrupted him, raising his forefinger and looking directly at Seán's parents. 'Your son hurt her in some way.'

Silence followed. Seán shook his head in disbelief, as his parents stared wide-eyed at Jack. He continued. 'Now, I wear a hearing aid, as you can see, so I didn't hear everything, but she cried out in pain. I heard that! She had a bandage on her arm too, completely defenceless.'

'So you didn't exactly see what actually happened?' Seán checked.

I didn't like this push towards a different direction from him.

'Jack was aware of me screaming in pain when you hit out at me and pushed me away.'

'You're putting words in his mouth, Cara.' Sean tried to remain calm, but his expression was filled with tension.

'No, no, in fairness, the young lady has done nothing wrong. It happened like she said. I offered her my support and I stand by it. I've seen enough abuse in the back of my taxi over the years.'

'Thank you, Jack, I appreciate that,' I responded.

George spoke now. 'Did Mrs Cawley offer you anything in return for your "support"?'

'How dare you!' I was horrified. And to think, I gave him credit for seeming like a nice old man.

'No, she didn't. Nothing like that, no,' Jack insisted. 'In fact, I have your behaviour from that night on video.' He took out his phone and showed the incriminating six-second video of Seán stumbling and cursing aggressively after he exited the taxi. I was even shocked to see him behave in this manner, despite bearing witness to it on the night in question. It was so out of character for him.

'Okay, Mum, Dad, let's just go now. I think we should end this here.' Seán gestured with his hand. I noticed the colour draining from his face too. He looked as if he might faint. At least if he did, there would be a doctor present.

'Yes, love, we've heard enough,' May said softly on seeing that her son was visibly shaken.

They left, comforting Seán and patting him on the back. I wondered why they seemed to have so much faith in him, despite the evidence against him. That must be what unconditional love feels like. What a close family, I thought, as tears sprang to my eyes.

Jack noticed that I was upset.

'Are you okay? They only support him because they're his parents, that's all. That's what parents do for their kids, y'know.'

'Yes, I suppose so,' I sobbed, as an unexpected pang of grief for my own mother pierced my heart. 'It's just that my own mother passed away and we were very close.' Jack said nothing, but looked sympathetic. If only Mother were here now to support me, the way Seán had his parents, I wept to myself. I was suddenly overcome with such pain that I dropped to my knees without thinking.

Jack rushed over to help me up. I thanked him and pulled myself together. He had to get back to work. He squeezed my hand and told me to mind myself. His kindness only made me cry more, as I wiped streaks of black from my cheeks. That bloody mascara, I thought. It's really not worth it. I cleaned up in the grimy train station toilets and began to make my way home.

I wondered if Declan would support me now, in my hour of need. I questioned if our love was unconditional. I was aware I was in his good books for overlooking his infidelity with Bernadette. I liked that he saw it as me being charitable and forgiving. I liked the idea of him seeing me in that light.

I was really only looking at the bigger picture, knowing that we'd need Bernadette and her cheap childcare services when she got back on her feet. I felt no jealousy either, as I knew she was no competition for me. If I wanted that sort of attention from Declan, all I'd have to do was step up and make an effort. That would make him forget Bernadette for good. He would choose me over her in a heartbeat. Their shared love of the GAA was no competition for our shared creation of Lucy. Was it? Damn, I let a little doubt seep in. Anyway, no point in bearing a grudge, I decided, as the grudge I bore against Sean was currently all I could handle.

The next challenge I would face was going back to work on Monday. On one hand, I was dreading it, but on the other, I was ready. I felt fierce. The nervous breakdown seemed like a lifetime ago. Nothing could ever break me like that again. I wasn't going to let those HR swats get to me. I'd show them some life skills I'd been perfecting during my time off. Yes! I was ready to face those beasts!

✧   ✧   ✧

'HI CARA! WELCOME back! You look great!' I got a similar welcome from everyone, but knew full well that Linda had been instrumental in the warm welcome I received. She, very thoughtfully, rang me the night before to give me some encourage-ment-'Walk in with your head held high. You deserve respect. You've recovered gracefully from an illness. And remember, I've got your back.'

Funny how things worked out for the best. Linda had come through for me as a reliable, knowledgeable confidante and supporter. In fact, I couldn't imagine a better doctor! She didn't put pressure on me to further pursue matters regarding Seán and what I'd confided with her. She believed that I was engaging in talk therapy and seeking legal advice. She believed me because that's what I told her. She said she trusted I would deal with it and seemed content to allow me to get on with matters without her intervention. It made for an easier relationship for both of us. I didn't have to explain what I was actually doing to Seán and she didn't have to get involved with all that paperwork and hassle of reporting a colleague to the council.

As the day wore on, no one gave me extra work to do, or even mentioned staying late or working the odd weekend. If they did, I'd tell them where to go and I think they knew it. I had an air of confidence about me that they weren't used to. I was aware that I had appeared unhinged on previous occasions while visiting the office for doctor's appointments, but never realised the legacy that would afford me. Many of the staff actually seemed to be intimidated by me now and I had somehow garnered a newfound respect.

Barbara was a bit standoffish too and left me alone. Rumour had it that she had her own personal problems and was also availing of Linda's services regularly. Oh yes! The job finally made her crack. Barbara was at the top of her game in HR, but there was a price to pay for all these promotions and by the look of her, she was paying it now. Ha! I chuckled to myself.

I didn't reach out to Barbara in any way, as I'd never felt much warmth from her in the past. I did, however, leave a few extra folders on her desk, when no one was looking. I wasn't going to give that insincere cow any special treatment, just because she was currently a bit down in the dumps. In fact, I didn't feel even a shred of sympathy for her and emphatically believed that I was indeed acting in a perfectly reasonable manner. What was it that Jack, the taxi driver, had said? '*What goes around comes around.*'

Chapter Eighteen

WORK, THESE DAYS, was a breeze for me. I walked all over everyone and they seemed to be afraid of me. My time off had gained me a newfound respect that I never thought possible. Turns out, being weird and unhinged pays dividends. Who knew?

Barbara, on the other hand, was but a shadow of her former self. Rumours spreading around the office implied that it wouldn't be long before I would be taking over as boss. She was having regular meetings with the in-house doctor and she mentioned something about possibly going on stress leave. I relished my new status as top dog in the office and had even started to meet Linda for coffee in a non-corporate environment. Just a chat with a new friend, a real friend, someone who understood me.

I never mentioned the fact that I was screwing with Seán's medical career. I felt as though I could handle this one on my own. I also worried that Linda might disapprove of me putting a fellow doctor's career in jeopardy. I tried to glean some info about Barbra's plans, but Linda, being the true professional, gave nothing away.

I accompanied Declan and Lucy into the hospital to visit Bernadette on a few more occasions. I noted her look of trepidation whenever I entered the ward with them, but we were always polite to each other like good neighbours. We avoided any talk of the delicate circumstances of her fall from the couch, or as I referred to it in my mind, her fall from grace.

We talked about my return to work, Lucy's schooling and general chit chat about the weather and GAA. I was relieved to hear Bernadette's positivity in relation to the future care of Lucy. The current creche fees were astronomical, but Lucy was thriving in this state-of-the-art facility, mixing with Ireland's elite. It was a fantastic short-term option for us, even though it was a bit far away. However, we wouldn't be able to afford it for much longer, so everyone involved hoped for a speedy recovery for Bernadette, albeit with varying motives behind the good wishes.

I got home from work to an empty house, as Declan was collecting Lucy and stuck in traffic. I got a fright when my phone rang, but had my prepared response for after-hours work calls ready—'*Please do not call me after hours. I have clocked off and this is my personal time. Refer to*

Barbara with your query, thank you.' After a quick rehearsal in my head, I promptly realised on answering that it wasn't work calling. It was Seán.

'Seán?'

'Yes, it's me. Hello, Cara.'

'Yes?' I snapped, trying to refreeze my quickly melting heart.

'Look, I don't know how far you've gotten with proceedings against me, but myself and my parents would like to ask you not to go ahead with them...'

'Oh really!'

'Yes, yes, if there's any way we could settle this ...'

'Oh, you'd just love that, wouldn't you! An out-of-court settlement, pay me for my silence!'

'Cara, please hear me out. I know you'll see sense. My parents thought you were a perfectly reasonable person.'

'Did they?' I was stunned to hear that. I'd assumed his parents would hate my guts.

'Yes, we talked about it and we'd like to offer you a sum of money to avoid the stress of the legal system.'

'The stress for you or me? I know I've done nothing wrong, so I don't feel stressed about it.'

'Okay, I meant to avoid the stress for everyone. If we could come to some sort of an arrangement, maybe?'

'Well, you already know I have some debts I'd like to pay off.'

'Yes, I remember our conversations.'

Silence.

'Cara, would ten thousand euros help with those debts?'

'Haha, is that what your Mammy and Daddy are willing to offer?'

Seán seemed embarrassed into silence.

I continued confidently. 'Seán, I think you have no idea what I could actually get from this if it goes to court. You are seriously underestimating the sum, so based on your offer, I will decline. In fact, I've a meeting booked with my lawyer for tomorrow afternoon. I've been getting some advice, you know, from the legal eagles down at the club ...'

'The club?'

'Oh, yeah, the GAA club. My husband is very involved.'

'Your husband? I thought you were separated?'

Ooops, I'd forgotten about that. I made a mental note to purchase a 'Little White Lies' notebook to keep track of my innocent, harmless untruths.

'Oh yes, we were going to separate and then, well, when he saw how upset I was after the assault, he decided he wanted to take care of me and we made a decision for the sake of our daughter to get back together.'

'I see. I certainly wouldn't call it an assault, though,' Seán was starting to sound sceptical now and I sensed it.

'Yes, Declan is a senior member of the club and there are a number of solicitors and trainee solicitors amongst his closest friends. You know, some are wives or partners of members, but it's such a tight-knit, close community that everyone helps each other out.'

Seán didn't reply, but I thought I heard a sigh. I was starting to get desperate.

'Oh, obviously I haven't mentioned any names, yet. I mean, people don't even know the legal advice we're seeking is for me. Up to now, I've been letting on it's for a friend at work, just to protect your identity, for the time being anyway. You know, a lot of them could be patients of yours.'

Still no reply from Seán, which made me feel increasingly uneasy.

'I've also become very friendly with Linda recently, since she stopped seeing me as a patient. Very friendly indeed. We just had coffee yesterday in Reny's. You know that new coffee shop on Balfe Street?'

Yes, that had done the trick. Now I could hear the fear return to his voice.

'Look, I don't know how much money you think I have, but I've only been practising as a GP for less than three years and I'm still repaying university loans.'

'Yeah, sure you are! I'm also sure George and May repaid all your educational loans. I have no doubt about that!'

This time, his heavy sigh was loud and clear. He was buckling.

'Look, Seán, I know exactly what you're at risk of losing if I go through with this court case. I just need to figure out how much your career in medicine means to you. How about adding another zero to that 10k?'

'Cara! No! You're way off track now, no way!'

'Yes way! I can see how much you want to end this without being named in court publicly. I'm totally serious, one hundred grand and you won't hear from me again.'

'Jesus Christ! You must be out of your mind if you think I could pay you a sum like that. I'll take my chances in court!'

Oh no. I needed to act fast. 'Are you sure about that, Seán?'

He hesitated.

'Tell me, what was your final offer going to be? Surely, you didn't think for a minute that I'd accept a measly 10k!'

'Fifteen thousand. That's as high as I'm pre-pared to go.'

'Eighty thousand is as low as I'm prepared to

go!'

'For Christ's sake, do you even know what you're doing?'

'Did you, when you carelessly struck me in the cab? No one will believe you, once that video is shared.'

Seán took a deep breath. I could hear it. 'Twenty thousand and that's my final offer!'

'Seventy-five, and this will all go away.'

'No, no, that's too much.'

'Really? I would have thought a career in medicine would be worth a lot more than that! C'mon, Seán, I know you can go higher. Wouldn't "Mummy and Daddy" help you out?'

'Twenty-five, and that's my final offer.'

'No way! You make twenty-five grand in a few month's work! That's bullshit! I'm hanging up! I'll see you in court!'

'Cara! Wait!'

I barked at him. 'Only if you double it!'

He didn't respond, so I waited. Silence. The silence was promising, I thought. Then, I whispered, 'I'm glad we're doing this over the phone. I know what you're capable of.'

'Cara, that's not fair and you know it.'

'It's my word against yours and I have both evidence and a witness prepared to testify. I know my GP, Linda, would back me up too if it came to it. She'd have to. Face it, you have a hell of a lot more to lose than me, Seán. Just accept it.'

Silence.

He eventually surrendered. 'Ok, ok, you win. I'll pay.'

Time to confirm. 'Fifty thousand, yes?'

'Yes,' he said in a sorrowful voice, like in a '*how has my life come to this*' kind of way.

'I want that in writing. If I don't have it by tomorrow morning, I'll keep my appointment with my solicitor at three o'clock. Got it?' I lied through my teeth, but he didn't know that. He had no idea what I was or wasn't capable of. Neither did I, come to think of it.

'Yes, and I'll require evidence that the video hasn't been shared and that it's deleted.' Seán replied. It sounded like he was welling up now.

I hung up swiftly. I suppressed any feelings of sympathy towards him, insisting to myself that he really did hurt my arm that night—yes, he really did! And he shouldn't have done that. He should have been more careful.

I knew deep down that he didn't do it intentionally and that my pride was more wounded than my arm, but I still required revenge nonetheless. All those plans I had made in my head to share a future with him. I had fallen in love with him, hook, line and sinker. I would have dumped Declan for him without a second thought. I'd often imagined Seán lifting Lucy with his strong, defined, fair-haired, muscular arms. How could he treat me like that? How could he? I escaped the rising guilt in my gut by reassuring myself that his haughty, upper class parents would most likely foot every cent of the bill.

✧　✧　✧

TWENTY MINUTES LATER, I was still shaking after the phone call. I didn't know what to do with myself, so I made tea and opened a tin of biscuits. As soon as I sat down on the chesterfield to decompress, Declan walked in.

'Oh! What are you doing at home? I thought you were going to the hospital.'

'I did. They wouldn't let me in.'

'What do you mean?'

'Well, remember I mentioned Bernadette had picked up a fierce chesty cough?'

'No.'

He raised his eyes. 'Well, I did. I definitely told you. Sure, you never listen! Anyway, the cough turned into a chest infection and now she's got pneumonia. Poor divil!'

'Gosh! You think you're going to get better in the hospital, not worse.'

'We were only joking about that last week, but that was when we thought it was just a harmless cough. It's gone into her chest and lungs now. No visitors until the infection clears. She'll be lonely as hell, she will, you know how she loves the bit of company.'

Now it was my turn to raise my eyes. 'Hmm, I do indeed. Look, Declan, I'm glad you're home early. I wanted to talk to you about something.'

'Sounds serious. Everything okay?' He went to the fridge to check what he felt like. He grabbed a carton of chicken soup.

'Decant that first, Declan, before you microwave it.'

'Hmm, what?'

'Decant it into a bowl. Here, let me,' I offered.

'It's not a fine wine, Cara. I've said it before, you've got notions, you do.'

'Anyway, as I was saying. I've something to tell you. Sit down on the chesterfield and I'll bring this over on a tray for you.'

He washed his hands and did as he was told. As I prepared his supper, I rehearsed in my head how I would play this one. Whatever I shared, it was imperative that he approved of every decision I'd made thus far. It was perfectly reasonable to rely on my husband's support in a time of crisis like this. I was pretty sure of that.

Chapter Nineteen

I PLACED HIS bowl of soup on our portable lap table, which had been Declan's Christmas present this year. I went to the fridge to retrieve the can of Guinness I'd hidden behind the free range chicken. I wanted to surprise him. I urged him to sit up straight before placing it on his lap.

'Oh, you're buying Guinness now? Trying to compete with the treatment I got next door, are you?' As soon as he said it, he regretted it and lowered his eyes. I decided to let it go, considering what I was about to impart with him. I went to the cupboard, got him a pint glass and placed it on the tray.

'Is that so I can decant the Guinness?' he chuckled.

'Declan, pay attention now. Something happened recently that I didn't tell you about. Remember Doctor Seán, the one I used to have the phone consultations with?'

'I do, yeah. You were mad about him. You were raging when he turned you over to Linda.'

'Well, not quite, but anyway, I bumped into him on my night out in town in mid December. Remember I met Margot for Christmas drinks?'

'Eh no, I thought it was Beatrice you were meeting. Isn't that what you said?'

Oh, where is the *Little White Lies* notebook when I need it?

'Oh yes, actually I think you're right. Maybe I just happened to bump into Margot or something and that's why I got mixed up. It doesn't matter anyway. The point is, I bumped into Doctor Seán in the taxi queue and he was drunk and he tried to kiss me.'

'Hahaha! You're joking! Sure, he's only a young lad!'

'He's thirty-one actually and it's not like I'm old!'

'Sure, you're forty!'

'I'm not quite forty yet, Declan! And, according to my self-help books, "*Life begins at forty*", so you know, it depends on how you look at it. Anyway, the point I'm trying to make is, he was drunk and a little rough with me and he hurt my arm.'

'Why didn't you tell me this at the time?'

'I thought you'd be mad that we kissed.'

'Wait, you said he *tried* to kiss you. Did you kiss him back?'

'Well, I … I got a shock, that's all, so I didn't

pull away immediately.'

'Oh yeah, I'm sure you didn't!'

'Declan, for goodness sake! I'm trying to tell you something really important here! I was mad at him for pushing me and hurting my arm and ...'

'Surely, that was an accident. I mean, he wouldn't have pushed you on purpose! I spoke to him on the phone many times about your drug addiction and honest to God, he was the perfect gentleman. Couldn't do enough for ...'

'It wasn't an addiction. I merely had a penchant for sleeping pills. It's very innocent when you think about it. I mean, who doesn't like a good night's sleep? Anyway, that's by the by. Now, just listen to me, okay? I was mad that he hurt me and I told him I was thinking about bringing him to court. That's when he buckled and offered me a sum of money to keep quiet.'

'Holy God, Cara! What have you been getting yourself into?'

'I've accepted his offer, and just so you know, you're not allowed to breathe a word of this to anyone, right? No one must know, or I'll have to give all the money back and actually go through with a court case.'

'Cara, we wouldn't have the money to pay a lawyer and all that. It costs a fortune, you know!'

'Yes I do, and fortunately the matter is settled now and we don't have to.'

'So wait a sec, did he not claim it was an accident? Why did he just offer you a pay off? I don't get it.'

'There was a witness, you see. Someone who saw him mistreating me and was willing to testify in court. I think that scared him off and he realised he was in the wrong.'

'Who was it? Beatrice?'

'What? Who? No! It was the taxi driver.'

'Are you saying you were in a taxi with him?'

'Hmmm? Oh yes, we were going in the same direction, so it made sense. You know how expensive taxis are!'

'So, you're telling me that this guy tried to kiss you, then pushed and hurt you, while being blind drunk and you thought it would be a good idea to get into a taxi with him? Something doesn't add up here! You're not telling me the full story! Were you planning to go home with him?'

'Of course not! No! Sure, I had a broken arm, Declan! Don't be daft! I made a bad decision. I thought I'd be safe in a taxi and I just wanted to get home. The queues were mad that night with all the Christmas revellers. Anyway, he was still intoxicated in the taxi and he sort of lunged at me and I got a terrible fright. The taxi driver was concerned about me and gave me his card in case I wanted to press charges and needed a witness. Seán later realised this could jeopardise his medical career, so he paid me to keep quiet about the whole thing.'

'Ah, for the love of ... This is, this doesn't make ... I can't believe I'm only hearing about this now, when everything is done and dusted.'

'I just never found the right time to tell you.'

'How much did he give you?'

'Ten thousand!'

'Ten thousand euros? Bloody hell!'

'I know! Great, isn't it? I'm going to start settling some of our loans as soon as I can get to a bank.'

Declan leaned back on the couch in disbelief. He put the tray down on the floor and ran through the course of events, audibly muttering to himself. I picked up his tray and pottered around in the kitchen. I could hear him. 'No, it doesn't add up ...' Every muscle in my body tensed up, but I chose to carry on the pretence that I couldn't hear him.

I made a little noise with the delf while loading the dishwasher. I really didn't want him to question me any more about it. I vowed to get that *Little White Lies* notebook up and running as soon as Declan left the room. It was imperative now. I was losing track big time. I'd get myself in hot water if I wasn't careful. I sat at the kitchen table and opened up the laptop to type up some reminders and just simply appear busy. He looked my way, with a face full of scepticism. And that's when I got an idea to distract him!

'What are you doing now, Cara?' he asked with a raised eyebrow, like a sleuth.

'Hmm, oh, just looking up holidays. You know there's sun in Lanzarote all year round! It's twenty-one degrees there at the moment!'

He immediately perked up. 'Ah, it's been so long since we had a holiday, that sounds amazing!' This was too easy. Then, I had an even better idea.

'Oh, well now, I was just looking for me and Lucy. Sure, you couldn't leave poor old Bernadette alone in the hospital, could you?'

'Who? What? Ah well now, she's in the infection control unit. She'll be there for at least a week to shake this one off, but you know, it always takes longer than they say, doesn't it? And, with no visitors permitted, there's nothing I can do for her now.'

'Ah, the poor thing. My heart goes out to her,' I channelled Barbara's fake tone of concern for that one. Sure, I'd learned from the best.

'Ah, never a truer word was spoken, never a truer word. Now, listen, book me in too for Lanzarote. You might as well. Bernadette won't even know I've gone. She's dosed up on antibiotics and steroids. I'll visit her first thing when we get back. Any last-minute deals there?'

'Yes, there's a package deal leaving next Tuesday for a week. Only 2,200 half board, in a hotel in Playa Blanca, right by the beach!'

'Well, I'm due a fair amount of time off work. Hardly took any holidays last year and they let me carry over a few days. What about you?'

'Oh, I'll get my days off. Any protests and I'll just get Linda involved and tell her it's for my mental wellbeing. She can pull a few strings for me. She's great like that!' I beamed.

'Is she? That sounds a bit corrupt to me, but what do I know! And what about Lucy missing school?'

'Sure, she's flying it academically. They do so much ancillary work with her in that new creche that I think she's covered half the curriculum before they even start it in school. Will I book it?'

'One week from Tuesday, let's see now …'

'Oh wait!'

'What? What is it now?'

'It says here, it's the same price for two weeks! Can you believe that? Talk about a bargain!'

Declan sank lower in his chair and looked up, wide-eyed.

'Two weeks for the price of one, sipping cocktails in the sunshine by the beach. Now that sounds like a perfectly reasonable offer! Book it, Cara! I'm in!'

Chapter Twenty

TWO WEEKS IN the glorious Canarian sunshine was just what the family needed. Lucy was in her element, meeting playmates at the pool and on the beach. There were so few children there at this time of year, that whoever she met, instantly became a best buddy.

Lucy and I went for walks on the beach, collecting shells and examining our footprints, while Declan stole away regularly to O'Shaughnessy's Irish Bar to discuss the latest match in great detail with the punters. I shopped till I dropped, having received the cheque from Seán two days before our departure. I mainly invested in oversized sunglasses and elegant sun hats to protect my precious face from ageing in the sun. Those three crinkly lines above my left eye hadn't disappeared yet and seemed to be deepening by the day. I was concerned about them. The deeper they got, the more determined I became to find a way of removing them. They made me look furrowed and angry, even when I was feeling light and joyous. How dare they!

We enjoyed luxurious meals every night over-looking the beach. Declan worried that I was getting back to my old spending habits and warned me that the 10K would be blown in no time, but I insisted there was enough and lied that all my purchases were *'cheap as chips'*. I also informed him that I was fairly confident I would soon be eligible for promotion at work. Declan didn't want any arguments on our holiday, so didn't protest too much. He'd rather spend this precious fort-night in ignorant peace, which made for a very harmonious family holiday!

Two weeks later, on a Tuesday afternoon, we arrived home exhausted and noticed a strange car parked in Bernadette's driveway.

'Oh! She must be home!' I exclaimed, hoping she would be able to resume childminding duties.

'Whose car is that?' Declan wondered.

'Look Declan, I'm sure Bernadette has other trusty contacts apart from you who can give her a lift when she needs it!' It had been a source of stress for him that Lucy had buried his phone in the wet sand as a 'joke' on the first day of our holiday and it wouldn't turn on as a result. Mine had no credit and although I kept promising to get some so Declan could make a few calls, I just never got around to it. There was always something more exciting to do in Lanzarote!

Still in the driveway, we started to unpack the car when Bernadette's sister, Siobhán, came out from next door and approached us.

'Haven't you heard?' she asked with a sombre expression.

'Siobhán! How are you? Nice to see you again! We've just been away on a little family holiday, much overdue! Wouldn't you agree, Cara?' Declan winked and I noticed the healthy glow of colour on his temple.

However, our smiles narrowed when we registered the solemn look on Siobhán's face.

'She, she passed away in hospital ... last week.'

'What? Bernadette?' Declan squealed.

'Yes, Declan. She asked for you in her dying words. I was with her and she mentioned you.'

Now it was my turn. 'I don't understand! How did she ...?'

'She contracted MRSA in the hospital and her system was so weak with the pneumonia, she ... she couldn't fight it.'

Siobhán teared up.

'Jesus Christ, I don't believe it!' Declan reached his hands to his head.

Lucy got involved. 'Is Bernie dead?'

I picked her up and took her inside. Declan stayed in the front garden chatting with Siobhán. It took me a half-hour to calm Lucy down. She was exhausted after the flight anyway, so I put on some cartoons and wrapped her in a blanket on the couch in the end. The TV distracted her at least. Declan came in looking as white as the crisp, linen sheets on the hotel bed in Lanzarote. He'd lost his beach glow already. He sat down and put his head in his hands. I approached him.

'I can't believe it, Declan. I just can't believe she's gone. Lucy was so upset. I think she wore herself out with tears.'

'Siobhán said her dying words were '*is that you, Deckie?*'' Declan sobbed.

'Deckie? Did she really call you Deckie?' I was taken aback, but he ignored me and continued.

'Siobhán said the pneumonia shattered her. She got a call advising her not to book her return trip home to the UK, once Bernie contracted the hospital infection. She knew straight away it was serious. They only allowed her to see Bernie for a few minutes at a time. She had to wear a medical mask and gloves. That must be why Bernie didn't recognise her. She thought it was me. She thought I'd come to see her.' He broke down, uncontrollably.

'Oh God, Bernie, my Bernie!' he sobbed.

'Your what? Declan, pull yourself together. It's not your fault. You weren't to know her infection would get so serious. How could you have known?' I reached over and patted his back. He turned and held me. Tight. We stayed like that for a few minutes. I think the holiday brought us closer together. And now this.

'My damn phone,' he said. 'I should have bought a new one over there, or tried to get it fixed. Siobhán tried to contact me to let me know. She said she tried ringing you too, Cara.'

'Oh, I never answer if I don't recognise the number. I usually assume it's work and I certainly didn't want to be bothered on the holiday. Sorry, Declan.'

'Oh. You shouldn't do that. You should always answer in case of emergencies,' he admonished.

I put my head down. 'Yes, yes you're right. I will from now on.'

'Siobhán said the funeral was small, only a few neighbours and some of Roger's people. It was a beautiful service, but small … you know. She said there just wasn't time. It all happened so fast.'

'Poor Siobhán. I suppose that was a lot of pressure on her and she wouldn't know many people around here, what with living in the UK most of her life. When did Bernadette say she moved?'

'Hmm? Oh, way back. She was barely twenty, I think, when she got the boat over.'

All this talking seemed to be helping Declan pull himself together. He was perking up a bit and the colour returned to his cheeks.

'Siobhán asked why Bernie only mentioned me. She thought you two had a falling out or something, especially when you didn't answer your phone.'

'Oh? What did you tell her?'

'Ah, just that she would have known me better as I dropped off Lucy and collected her most days. That's all.'

'Good. That's the truth too.'

'She's tidying up Bernie's things and planning to go back to the UK soon. She mentioned something about forms I needed to see or something. I'm not sure what she was on about. I'll see her before she goes.'

Declan got up and went into the kitchen. He opened a bottle of whiskey. It had been a Christmas present from the club to thank him for his coaching. He sat down at the kitchen table and drank it, neat. He ignored Lucy's howls when she awoke. He said he couldn't comfort her now, so I went to her to calm her down. It had been a long flight. We were all shattered. Soon Lucy stopped crying and we realised she must have cried herself back to sleep again. He cursed himself to no end for missing those calls while we were away. I tried to be sympathetic and was glad he didn't turn on me for ignoring Siobhán's calls. He drained the bottle of whiskey and lay on the couch.

I went out to the car and lugged in all the heavy bags and suitcases. I don't think he heard me. I unpacked everything and stuck on a load of laundry. I checked on Lucy too. She was sleeping soundly, and then Declan. He had passed out on the couch. The whiskey had done what he wanted it to do. I left a note on the table in case he woke up and then nipped out to the local shop.

Declan and Lucy slept through the night. Lucky them—almost fourteen hours straight. I was dead jealous, but knew they both needed it badly.

I got up early and pottered about in the kitchen. Eventually, the familiar aroma of sizzling sausages woke Declan. He looked flabbergasted to see me cooking high fat, overly processed, only 52% pork sausages. Not even the expensive, premium ones with 80% pork that I just about tolerated once or twice a year. No, I bought the brand I knew he loved. They were the ones Bernadette used to cook for him. He followed his nose to the table. I put a plate of sausages in front of him and two slices of buttery toast. I hadn't seen him look so happy since, well … never! He looked like he'd just won the lotto, tearing into those sausages, and Lucy was over the moon too.

I stood in the kitchen admiring both of them tucking into their favourite breakfast and something happened to me. Deep within. All of a sudden. I don't know what it was. A kind of transcendence or something. I just instantly realised I had everything I'd ever wanted right in front of me. Why hadn't I realised this before now?

Why was I always running away? Looking for something or someone else? Declan cut the last sausage in two, so they could share it between them, and honestly, I felt like my heart snapped just as the sausage did. I dropped to my knees without warning.

'Mommy! Mommy!' Lucy shouted.

'Cara! What is it? What's wrong?' Declan rushed to my side on the kitchen floor. It all happened so fast that I couldn't express my true emotions. I couldn't find the words to say how I felt, so I just blurted out. 'Bernie! Ah, dear Bernie! I miss Bernie!' Lucy ran over then, with ketchup dripping from her chin. She knelt down beside us and the three of us held each other tight and cried together. Although I kept shouting Bernie's name, I knew deep down I was grieving for much more. More things, more people, more connections and dozens of missed opportunities.

We got showered and dressed and spent a few hours in the local park. Lucy was getting proficient at riding her bike without the training wheels now. I think she'd forgotten about her fall, our fall, at this stage. I hadn't. I was a nervous wreck trying to keep up with her, but Declan was on the other side, so that eased my nerves. He wouldn't let her fall. That, I knew for sure.

All three of us slept that night as if our lives depended on it. A solid twelve hours was slumbered by all of us, together in our bed with Lucy in the middle. I couldn't remember the last time I'd felt so well rested.

Both Declan and myself were relieved we had taken the next day off work. We had figured we'd need a day to unwind after the stress of a holiday. Yes, holidays, packing, flights etc.—it can be trying. We were right. We needed one more day before returning to the daily grind. We breakfasted again on sausages and toast, before going to visit Bernadette's grave.

A wooden cross had been erected in a mound of soil. She was buried alongside her beloved Roger, in his plot. Soon, her name would be engraved beside his onto the headstone. Grief overcame all three of us as we huddled together and bawled our hearts out at Bernadette's grave. Real, genuine, unruly tears. Lucy placed one of her favourite teddies on the grave, while I set down some flowers. Declan laid out a club jersey and a can of Guinness by the little cross—a perfectly reasonable tribute to his beloved Bernie. Then, we drove home in silence.

Chapter Twenty One

THAT EVENING, BERNADETTE'S sister, Siobhán, called in as promised. She told us she would be travelling home to the UK soon.

'I tidied up as much as I could. I gave anything that looked sentimental to Roger's family. Well, that is, I packed them in a box and labelled it and rang them in the US and asked if they wanted it. They're getting back to me. They really seemed to have lost contact over the years, such a pity. I'm sure Bernadette would have loved it if they visited, but you know ...'

'If it's any consolation Siobhán, I can promise you, she wasn't lonely. She had a very close bond with Lucy and a close friendship with myself ... and ... Cara.' Declan looked my way. He continued. 'Bernie was busy most weekends living the life down in the club and walking the dog and ... oh ...the dog?'

'Yes, that's one of the reasons I'm here. Poor Rex has been in the kennels for weeks now. I wondered, considering Lucy was so fond of him, if you'd like to take him on?'

'Yes!' Declan and I responded in unison. It was possibly the first time we'd ever said anything in unison.

'Oh brilliant! Bernadette was right about you! *"Such caring neighbours"*, she used to say! And on that note, there's another reason I wanted to speak with you before I leave for the UK. Bernadette phoned me from the hospital a few weeks ago and told me she wanted to change her will. Roger had wanted their estate to be divided evenly amongst their family members and at the time, Bernadette had no objections. However, no one from Roger's side showed up for his funeral. They didn't make the trip over from the US, nor did they call her. All she got was a sympathy card in the post about five weeks after his passing. She was devastated at the time.'

'Yes, she mentioned that to me, Siobhán. She was fairly cut up about their lack of contact,' Declan offered.

'Yes, the poor thing. Anyway, the purpose of her phone call to me was to let me know how happy she'd been in recent months, minding Lucy and getting to spend quality time with yourself, Declan. Oh, I'm sure she meant you too, Cara, but I know you were under the weather and suffering with a broken arm, so maybe ...'

'It's okay, Siobhán, I had my own troubles and

yes, she did spend a lot of time with Declan and Lucy in my absence. It's no secret.'

'Indeed, she said they were like family to her and had grown so fond of them, I mean you, all of you, in recent months. She seemed to gain a new lease of life in your company.'

'It means a lot to hear you say that, Siobhán. She did enjoy life to the fullest before she broke her shoulder,' Declan caught my eye and I couldn't help feeling a flutter of guilt.

'Did she discuss with you the changes she wanted to make in her will?' Siobhán enquired.

Again, Declan and I answered in unison. 'Yes.' 'No.' This time with contradictory answers—funnily enough this HAD happened before! I looked wide-eyed at Declan. 'Oh, she did? You never told me!'

'No, I never liked that morbid talk. And she had just broken her shoulder, so I told her not to be silly, and that she had plenty of life left in her.' Declan bowed his head and wiped a tear.

Siobhán continued. 'I gave her the go ahead and she invited her solicitor into the hospital to consolidate the changes. I visited with him yesterday and she left us equal shares of her properties.'

'Properties???' we exclaimed, once more in unison.

'Yes, did she ever mention herself and Roger invested in a holiday home in Rosslare?'

'No, but now I remember they used to holiday quite a bit in Wexford. I didn't realise they owned a property down there,' I replied.

'Yes, I've holidayed there myself plenty of times. It's a beautiful little bungalow by the beach. They bought it for next to nothing when Roger retired. Of course, now you won't be surprised, it's worth a small fortune! Such a popular holiday destination, isn't it? Anyway, Bernadette didn't want to go there without Roger, so she'd been renting it out to a local family for the past year. A rental company manages it, so she probably wouldn't have mentioned it much.'

I had to ask a question. 'And, you said equal share of both properties?'

'Well, yes. However, in the will, it states only Declan's name. Look here, I brought a copy with me.' Siobhán showed us the will bequeathing everything jointly to Siobhán Bennett and Declan Cawley.

'I ... I don't know what to say. I'm flabbergasted! I know she mentioned it, but I didn't think she'd go through with it while in hospital. I can't believe she had the energy to organise all that from her hospital bed. Some woman, she was, good ole Bernie! She was some woman!' Declan looked heavenward as he reminisced, lovingly.

Then, he took a closer look at the document. 'Although, hang on there a sec. Is this a mistake?

Look at Bernie's date of birth—that can't be right. She was only in her mid sixties!' Declan volunteered, innocently.

Siobhán corrected him. 'No, Declan, she was my older sister. She was actually seventy-five.'

'What? You can't be serious!' exclaimed Declan. I had never seen his mouth hang open so wide. I couldn't contain my laughter.

'Wouldn't that make her older than your mother, Declan?' I just threw it in. As I said before, I'm always willing to help.

'Hah? I don't … I don't understand, why would she lie about that?' He was perplexed.

My eyebrows rose so high that it hurt my forehead. I lowered them again when I thought about my lined brow. No more raising or furrowing, I reminded myself, in my head of course. Siobhán just shrugged, disinterestedly.

I didn't know where to look. Another windfall in the same month as my 50k! I couldn't believe this. I excused myself and left the room, saying I'd better go and check on Lucy. I went straight to our bedroom and screamed uncontrollably into my pillow. 50k from Doctor Seán, an almost certain promotion for me in the pipeline and now, about a quarter of a million worth of property! I thought screaming into my pillow was a perfectly reasonable reaction to all this fantastic, unexpected news! So I did it again, and again, and then one more time, before returning demurely to proceedings in the kitchen.

✧ ✧ ✧

LUCY WAS OVER the moon with excitement about getting to keep Rex full time! She'd always wanted a dog of her own and now here was Rex, her favourite dog in the world and a befitting reminder of his owner, whom she had loved dearly.

She was equally excited about getting to remain in the elite, A-list creche, in which she had made loads of friends and learned more there through highly structured play routines than she'd ever learned in a day at school. And she loved travelling on the bus with her creche mates. She was mixing with the cream of the crop!

As for Declan, he seemed to be constantly signing paperwork to do with his 50% share of Bernadette's property. He travelled to Rosslare to see the holiday home as soon as the tenants moved out. He spent a few weekends down there on his own, claiming he wanted to fix up things in the house before putting it on the market. I was all for it, thinking the better it looked, the more it would increase the sale price.

As for me, I dwelled on my furrowed brow for far longer than I should have. I think it was the influx of new, younger staff joining the company that made me paranoid about my appearance. The young ladies in their twenties and thirties were all so fresh faced and vibrant looking. I felt, with my impending fortieth birthday, that I was in danger of losing my vitality. I concentrated so much on not furrowing my brow that I may have accidentally created more lines in the process of stretching it one way or another.

I noticed a new Botox clinic had opened up on the corner near our office. Linda disclosed to me that she'd booked an appointment, even though I couldn't fathom why. She was considerably younger than me and didn't have a visible line on her forehead. She maintained it was a preventative measure. She wanted to start before the lines set in. She was a doctor and knew her stuff, so I figured if it's good enough for her...

And of course, I had my secret stash of money now. I'd only disclosed 10k to Declan and that was well spent at this stage, but I had plenty of personal funds to play around with. The sale of Bernadette's properties could be used to eventually repay our loans, so my money was MY money! It was all mine!

I booked an appointment in *Raise That Brow Now* and flicked through the brochure while I waited to go in. 'Flattened foreheads guaranteed', it promised, as well as 'Walk taller, look higher'. Everything about it appealed to me. I was their target market. The right age, the perfect location and the stretchy purse strings!

My skin therapist mentioned wonderful things like 'dipping into my fountain of youth' and 'drowning my frowning', but I was utterly disappointed with the results in the end. Nothing happened! Just nothing! I looked the exact same. I searched my face for a mark or a bruise as proof that I'd had work done, but nothing. My forehead was not flattened and my wrinkles felt the opposite of relaxed. They were far more tense now. I could feel them and they hurt. I found I wasn't 'walking taller' or 'looking higher'. Instead I seemed to be frowning more and looking down.

I cancelled my next appointment in *Raise That Brow Now* and booked into *Lessen That Expression* instead. On the plus side, this clinic was considerably cheaper, but unfortunately located at the other side of town. The not-so-salubrious side, if I'm honest, but Mandy was great. She loved hearing how rubbish the other clinic was and reassured me that the same wouldn't happen in her clinic.

Holy hell, was she right! I looked like a cage fighter by the time I arrived home. Lucy screamed and Declan offered to call an ambulance. I had to book a few days off work until the swelling and bruising went down. I couldn't even collect Lucy from the creche bus for fear of being seen. It was a nightmare and I cursed Mandy to no end. I was now closer to the fountain of phantoms than the fountain of youth.

On a whim, the following day, I decided to drive down to Rosslare to see the bungalow Declan had been working on. I rang my mother-in-law, Cathy, and invited her over to help Declan take care of Lucy while I went away.

I knew we weren't going to keep the Rosslare bungalow, but I wanted to see it before it went sale-agreed. I packed an overnight bag and left a note on the kitchen table saying I was going into hiding for a couple of days. I could have texted Declan, but I knew he was mad busy at work. I deemed it perfectly reasonable to sneak away for a night or two, to allow my face to heal. I grabbed the Rosslare keys and the latest edition of *How To Look Ten Years Younger*, and set off on my road trip.

Chapter Twenty Two

I KNEW THE address off by heart, but when I arrived I got so confused. I wondered if I'd mixed up the numbers. Was it 12 Beach View or 21? It was just that neither bungalow had a For Sale sign. I contemplated ringing Declan to check if I was on the wrong track altogether, but there was no one around so I took a chance and stuck the key in the door of number 12. It opened. I knew I had the right address in my head, but why was there no For Sale sign outside? How would we ever repay our debts if he didn't sell this place quickly?

I entered and looked around. It was in perfect condition. Why had he been coming down so often to fix it up? He gave me the impression it was in need of some renovation, but it looked to me like it had been recently updated and well kept. I couldn't help but notice all the framed pictures of Bernadette on the table, shelves and mantelpiece. It appeared like a shrine to her.

Newspapers and GAA magazines were strewn across the coffee table and the fridge was well stocked with cans of Guinness. I spotted his toolbox beside the couch. I'd seen him pack it in the car to bring it down a few weeks ago. I wondered if I'd find evidence of what he'd been fixing up in there, but to my horror, it was empty! What was he playing at? Was this just a little escape for him to chill out, drink Guinness, watch sport and admire old photos of Bernadette in her heyday? What the heck was going on? Before I got a chance to plan my interrogation of Declan, my phone rang.

'Hi Declan.'

'Cara! I just read your note. How far down are you?'

'I've arrived.'

'Oh.'

'Where's the For Sale sign out front?'

'Yeah, I, em, haven't got around to putting it up yet.'

'Why not? What have you been doing?'

'Cara, I wish you gave me a bit of notice that you were going down there. I would have …'

'What?'

'I would have organised it for your visit and …'

'You probably would have hidden the cans in the fridge, put Bernadette's photos back in the box and filled your toolbox to pretend you had actually done something in the four weekends you spent down here ON YOUR OWN! Is that what you mean?'

'Look, I needed the time …'

'Time for what? You'd have more time in Dublin, without the five-hour round trip to Rosslare. What are you playing at, Declan?'

'I needed the headspace, okay. A lot has happened recently.'

'Are you pining after Bernadette or something? Do you come down here to grieve? Because that's what it looks like.'

'I wish we weren't doing this over the phone, but, yes I do miss her. We had a connection and …'

'And what? You don't have one with me?' I found that I was welling up now. I thought everything was finally going our way. We were a family again. I'd stopped my ridiculous obsession with Seán and well, we were rich now. What the hell else did we need?

'Cara? Are you okay?'

'I'm …' I reached my hand up to wipe away the tears and squirmed. 'Ouch.' I'd forgotten my face was in bits. It was so sore when I touched it. I caught my reflection in the mirror over the fireplace. *Oh Christ Almighty, what have I done to myself?*

'Are you okay, Cara?'

'I have to go, Declan. I'll just stay here tonight. I'll be back tomorrow and we can talk then. I promise.' I hung up.

Were we broken? *What's wrong with me that I hadn't noticed?* I sat on the couch, leaned back and tried to think. What was it that Declan had said to me last year? I'd shut him out once I had Lucy. I'd dismissed it at the time, but it had been nagging at me in the back of my mind. He'd said I had taken control of the care of Lucy when I was breastfeeding and wouldn't let him in. But I'd thought he was only dying to get back to the club and training and socialising. Was I wrong? Or did it just suit me to think that way? I lay down and thought some more.

Oooh, Bernadette's couch was comfortable. It was nowhere near as sophisticated as our chesterfield, but I couldn't sink into the chesterfield the way I could on this couch. That lady knew how to live. She had good insight into creature comforts— fried sausages, Guinness, home baking and ham sandwiches to make GAA matches more bearable. All the things Declan loved too. He didn't give a monkeys about the sophistication of our chesterfield. I'd say he loved this couch. He often complained that ours was too rigid. It's only now I see he had a point. I sank deeper.

Well, I knew I'd blanked him completely from my life when I became infatuated with Seán. That, I knew for sure. The beauty of Seán overshadowed everything else in my life. I see that now. Of course, I only do, because he didn't feel the same way. If Seán had matched my adoration for him, Lord knows where I'd be now. Probably in Trailers watching a band I cared little for, mingling with millennials I had nothing in common with and trying desperately to keep Seán from turning his head towards all the younger, more attractive versions of me. God, it sounds horrible. I'd never be content competing for his affections. And he'd never reciprocate my feelings for him. He was too young and handsome to get enraptured in me the way I would have demanded.

How come that realisation never entered my mind when I was in the thick of it? Hmmm, maybe the pills had something to do with that. Declan clocked it anyway. He knew straight away that I was chasing an unrealistic fantasy. He knew it was all in my head, but again, I didn't listen to him and only shared the saga when it had gone too far. I'm pretty sure he would have stepped in and defused the situation, before any money had exchanged hands. But I didn't let him in until it was too late.

I pictured Declan's face. His wide-eyed, curious expression lit up by his sky-blue, Irish eyes. It wasn't too late for me to win him over, was it? I massaged my forehead gently, and my fingers rolled delicately over the bulging creases. Up and down, up and down. Like my life thus far with Declan. Up and down. I assumed he'd forgiven me for my ridiculous infatuation with Seán and put it down to a midlife crisis, together with an unhealthy dependency on sleeping pills, antidepressants and benzos. *Oh lord, this sounds like I'm making excuses for my unreasonable behaviour and maybe I am. That's my prerogative, but perhaps Declan doesn't see it that way. I wonder how he evaluates the past year?*

I left my tender forehead and my fingers spread out over my crow's feet around my eyes. I wish I could say they were laughter lines, but no one in their right mind would believe it. I didn't have the capacity for belly laughter the way Bernadette did. I guess that's another thing Declan was attracted to. No, the lines around my eyes were purely stress-related and angst-ridden. How very unattractive, I surmised.

Declan said he needed time. That's why he came here alone. I can only presume it was time away from me he needed. I got up and grabbed a blanket from the hot press and lay down again on the comfy couch. I don't know why, but I placed my hand on my heart. Come to think of it, maybe it was something I'd read about in one of my self help books. *The Beast Within* had a heart, if I recall. I disregarded it at the time, but the sentiment obviously stuck with me.

This was the first time I'd ever tried to see things from Declan's point of view. An obvious failure on my part, as his wife and of course, the mother of his child. I tried hard to see me with Declan's eyes. Why hadn't I done this before? Perhaps if I had, I would have acknowledged other times when I excluded him. Like when the wonder of Baby Lucy consumed me. Declan felt it, but I couldn't see it. He was right. I'd shut him out then, just like I did when I was chasing Seán.

I pressed my resting hand to exert more pressure on my heart. I'd always been so dismissive of Declan and his needs. Maybe that's why he missed Bernadette. She listened to him, shared with him and laughed with him. I'd seen them together, easy in each other's company. Nothing was 'easy' with me. Nothing!

I caressed my resting hand and in turn, caressed my heart. Maybe being tactile with myself would encourage me to feel something. And to feel it deeper. Just like *The Beast Within*, I had a heart too. It was just difficult to find sometimes.

How could I expect Declan to be content, if I made everything so challenging for both of us? I really was the epitome of an imperfect, unreasonable wife. Despite that haunting thought racing through my mind, I somehow managed to drift off.

✧ ✧ ✧

I WOKE UP the next morning on the floor beside the couch. I must have rolled off in my slumber. I immediately panicked and did a few shoulder rolls to make sure I didn't suffer the same fate as Bernadette, but nothing seemed to be broken. Just my spirit.

Oh God, I was a terrible wife. Thoughts of my inadequate, defective 'wifeyness' had plagued me throughout the night. I think I dreamt Declan left me and the more I thought about it, the more I realised it actually could happen. Lucy was the only reason we were still together and although we both loved her dearly, that love alone wouldn't cement our union forever. Declan wouldn't put up with me. Why would he? It was true. I'd been an appalling wife to him, yet it dawned on me that I didn't want to lose him. I couldn't. I needed him.

The sudden realisation was like another hurley swing to my head. How could I have been so stupid? I channelled Scarlett O'Hara's resolve and clenched my fist with imaginary soil, chanting '*As God is my witness, I'll never be hungry again*'. I knew it was the wrong quote for my current situation, but it injected a powerful sense of determination into my psyche nonetheless.

I showered quickly and dashed out the door to find somewhere serving breakfast. I found a little coffee shop up the town and ordered a latte and a hot scone with jam and cream. The barista asked if I was coming from the Wexford Women's Refuge and it was only then that I remembered my bruised and battered face. I enquired about the location of the nearest chemist and bought some scar healing ointment, the same one I'd used after my fall in the park.

That made me remember how kind Declan had been to me back then and how he'd looked after me. I was struck by the memory of how he'd put me to bed after my breakdown at work and worried about me when I started popping this pill and that pill to help me sleep. Oh God, where would I be without him? He had my back. He looked after me no matter what dramatic, traumatic episode I found myself in. I had to get home.

Of course, when I arrived home, the house was empty. He was at work and Lucy was at school. I tidied the whole house from top to bottom and baked a lemon drizzle cake. I knew it was a favourite of both Declan and Lucy. I set *GAA Giants* to record later on, so Declan could watch it at his leisure. I thought that seemed like a perfectly reasonable gesture of goodwill towards my dear husband.

With my apron still on, semi covered in flour, I beamed in motherly, wifey welcomeness when they opened the kitchen door. Lucy screamed and Declan covered his eyes. "Jesus, Cara! Your face! It's gotten worse!" He proceeded to shield Lucy from the horror of me and they exited promptly. I mean, surely my face was worse than this when I fell in the park. This was a beauty procedure after all. I wasn't supposed to look like a freak.

I checked the kitchen mirror to see if their reaction was justified. Well okay, in fairness I was pretty badly bruised. I really wish I'd listened more to Mandy and read the after care instructions. I had no idea all the ibuprofen I was popping afterwards for my headache was actually going to increase the bruising. Lesson learned. Oh, where were they? Surely, they weren't so petrified that they'd refuse dinner. I went out to the hall to call them. I overheard Declan reassuring Lucy that *'honestly, it IS Mommy, I swear it's her'*. Oh no, not only was I an awful wife, but now an atrocious mother too. This quest for atonement wasn't going at all well.

They came down eventually and pushed around the food on their plates, all the while looking emotionally scarred. I apologised that I couldn't hide the bruising with makeup as it would only irritate the skin on my face, but reassured them it should disappear in a day or two. When they saw me tucking into my cottage pie, they joined me and ended up devouring every morsel. Lucy cheered up immeasurably when she saw the freshly baked lemon drizzle cake for dessert.

The meal was a success in the end, but Lucy didn't want me to put her to bed until my face healed, so I cleaned up while Declan did the tucking in.

When he came back, I had decanted a can of Guinness into a pint glass for him and had *GAA Giants* ready to play. He looked shocked.

'Are you going out or something?'

'Of course not, no, sure look at me! Where would I be going? Hahaha! No, I'm going to sit down beside you, my husband, and we're going to watch *GAA Giants* ... together!'

'What? You hate this show!'

'No, no, I don't hate it. I've just never given it a chance, that's all.'

'Cara, why would you even want to watch this? You've no idea who anyone is or what team they play for. You'll be thoroughly bored.'

'Declan, I had some time to think in Rosslare and I decided we don't spend enough quality time together. We don't have enough fun together.' I was starting to sound desperate now. He half-heartedly responded. 'No, we don't, do we?'

I sat beside him on the couch. 'I'm sorry for shutting you out when I was breastfeeding Lucy. You were right, I did. I shoved you back to the GAA, when you just wanted to spend time with us. I've come to the realisation that I can be a bit of a control freak and I wanted to control every part of Lucy's existence, without you, and I'm sorry for that.'

'Are you taking drugs again?'

'No. Why do you ask?'

'It's just, you've never apologised to me before ... for anything.'

'No, I don't suppose I have. Well, I'm trying to turn over a new leaf and become a better person. Maybe it's something to do with ageing and maturing and turning forty.'

'Another midlife crisis, is it?'

'Midlife enlightenment, actually. I read about it in one of my books.'

He didn't seem too impressed. His attitude was one of indifference. Had he stopped caring about me altogether?

'Declan, what did you do in Rosslare on your own?'

'I kicked back and relaxed. It's been a roller-coaster of a year. I just needed to unwind a bit.'

'And could you not have done that here in Dublin with Lucy and me?'

'No, I can't properly relax in your presence, Cara. I'm always on edge. It's hard to know what you're going to come out with next. You're very unpredictable and I'm very ... tired.'

'I see. Well, I agree I went a bit mad last year on the sleeping pills and Doctor Seán and all that, but I'm out the other side now, I promise.'

'Really? No more wild, ridiculous plans up your sleeve?'

'No.'

'What about your face? Are you going to continue with the botox? Is this your new addiction now that you're over the pills?'

'Well, I do worry about the amount of lines on my forehead. I worry about that a lot.'

'Don't you think all the worrying you do about it is creating more lines?'

'Em, I hadn't thought about it that way. But what if I look old before my time?'

'What of it?'

'Well, you won't want to be married to an old-looking woman, will you?' At that moment, I thought of Bernadette. I noticed Declan's eyes widened all of a sudden. No doubt the image of seventy-five-year-old Bernadette popped up in his mind too. He didn't respond. After a minute, I carried on.

'What did she have that I don't?'

'What did Doctor Seán have?'

Silence. He got me.

'Well, Cara? It's a perfectly reasonable question!'

Chapter Twenty Three

I DIDN'T WANT this to become about Seán and me. I wanted it to be about Declan and me. My husband. Only Declan.

'Look, that wasn't me. It was merely an infatuation. I blame my midlife crisis for all of that behaviour. I'm over it now, I swear.'

'I just can't believe you squeezed ten grand out of him for a drunken misunderstanding. I don't think you told me the full story. It doesn't add up.'

'Well, maybe I didn't share all the details, but it's in the past now.'

'And, you're using his hard-earned GP money to mess up your face in an attempt to change your appearance. It's not right, Cara, it's immoral.'

I put my head down. He was making me upset. I hoped I wouldn't cry, because that would hurt my already aching face. Tears would irritate the bruising.

'So, is there anything I can do now? Like, to redeem myself?'

'Give the money back. We don't need it. Once

next door sells, we'll be in for a windfall, well, I will be, anyway.'

'What do you mean? Aren't you going to share it with me? I booked our holiday to Lanzarote with my 10k. I shared it with the family.'

'I'll use it to pay off our debts. Then, we'll see.'

'What about Rosslare? Why aren't you trying to sell that?'

'I will, I will. It's just, I like going down there. It reminds me of …'

He got up and walked towards the kitchen. I could tell he was welling up.

'You miss her, don't you?'

'Of course I do.'

'You never answered my question. What has she got that I don't?'

He came closer and looked down on me, as I sat alone on the chesterfield. I looked up, meeting his eye as he loomed above. 'Strength of character, sense of humour, human decency and compassion.'

'Jesus Christ, Declan, that hurts! That really hurts!' I started to cry. 'Owwww.' I touched my face and immediately wished I hadn't. 'Owwww,' I bawled.

Declan remained calm. 'Are you crying because of what I said or because your face is sore?'

I looked at him. My forehead felt so tight, I wanted to pierce it open for relief. Then, maybe the bouncing ball that was causing my brain to throb incessantly would have an opening to jump out. Couldn't he see that I was in total agony? I reached out my hand towards him, but he didn't take it. I leaned over and fell off the couch onto my knees. He still didn't budge. He didn't rush to my side like he did when Bernadette fell off the couch. 'Which is it?' he demanded, still towering above me.

'Both! It's both, Declan!' I grabbed the leg of his jeans and yanked at it, still whimpering in pain. Eventually, I calmed myself down, while stretched on the cold, solid wooden floor. He was looking at me, with a serious, pitiful expression.

'Say something, Declan! For God's sake, say something!'

'Is this the end of it, Cara? I can't take any more of the drama. Promise me, this is it.'

I pulled at the denim material on the leg of his jeans and kissed it, while rubbing his socked feet with my other hand. Desperate times called for desperate measures and I seriously wanted to show him some affection at that moment. Kissing the leg of his ten-year-old, rarely washed, work jeans was pushing the boat out for me.

'Yes, yes, I promise. I'll be a changed woman from now on. I'll be all those things you say I lack. Well, maybe not the sense of humour. You either have that or you don't, but I'll work on my character and humanity. I can do that. I'm going to be a perfectly reasonable human being from now on.' Still on my knees, rubbing his socked feet, I looked up into his pained, blue eyes. 'I don't want to lose you, Declan.'

With that, he crouched down, picked me up and placed me on the couch. He switched the TV channel and dropped the remote on the couch beside me.

'I don't feel like watching *GAA Giants* with you. I'm going for a pint. I need to think.'

'To think about me, Declan? About us?'

He turned and looked at me with jaded eyes. 'To think about what's best for Lucy and me, from here on. I'll consider that first, before I think about you.'

He left me alone on the chesterfield. I jumped when I heard the front door closing. He's gone, I thought. Have I lost him? He's finally had enough of me. I pondered my behaviour in recent years. The smugness I'd felt of being in total control of Lucy's upbringing. On so many occasions, I'd simply fobbed Declan off, as if he meant nothing to us. I'd ignored the fact that it was him affording me the time and funding to indulge Lucy's every whim. I begrudged family days out, especially GAA days and most of Declan's other suggestions, in favour of high-end retail outlets and expensive coffee houses. All the things I knew Declan had no interest in.

I remained on the couch, thinking and despairing at the idea that my husband might leave me. If he did, I knew he'd meet someone else. There were a good few ladies at the club that had their eye on him. It wasn't just Bernadette that had been taken in by his charms. And, I thought about myself, there was certainly no hope in hell that I'd meet anyone else. Look what a mess I'd made of my last romantic pursuit. It almost ended in a court case and we were never even a couple, only in my wildest dreams and imaginings. No, I would be a spinster forever, while Declan would remarry some caring, good-natured GAA-loving nurse. She'd make a tremendous stepmother and I'd have to beg and plead with Lucy to spend time with me every now and then.

This future that I imagined seemed so realistic and it would be all my fault if it ever came to pass. Acting on an immature crush on my doctor, exaggerating mental illness symptoms to wrangle more time off work and neglecting the care of my precious daughter by disrupting her childcare routine when she was perfectly happy at Emma's. All for selfish reasons. Declan was right. I lacked compassion. I switched off the TV and went to bed, where a torturous night of tossing and turning awaited me. I heard him come in at midnight and he went straight to the spare room.

Thoughts of Declan plagued me into the morning light. I couldn't let him leave me. Our perfect little family must remain intact. I vowed to find a way, but no elaborate plan came to mind. I had nothing. All my plotting that used to come so naturally was exhausted. Drained of ideas, with zero options left, my only tactic now was to simply hope that Declan would find a way to forgive me.

✧   ✧   ✧

I STILL COULDN'T go into work with this botched Botox job, but realised I'd need a sick cert if I stayed off another day following annual leave. Well, I couldn't exactly go to Doctor Seán or even his clinic for that matter and I didn't want to go to Linda because it meant traipsing through the office. I rang her anyway to see what she'd recommend.

'Cara, if you're feeling fit and well, just come in to work. No need to be self-conscious. Everyone's so busy around here, they won't even notice.'

'Oh believe me, they will! Lucy is traumatised, the poor thing. Linda, I did something really stupid and took ibuprofen for my headache after the Botox. I didn't realise it would compound the bruising so much.'

'Oh Cara, that's exactly what you're not supposed to do. How could you not know that?'

'I had other things on my mind when the therapist talked about after care and then I didn't read the leaflet either. It's my own fault entirely, that's why I took the Monday and Tuesday off as annual leave. I really thought my face would improve, but it's still tender. I can't put makeup on to conceal it. Will I send a photo, Linda?'

'Okay, let's say we had a video call.'

I sent the photo and Linda sent back her deepest sympathy and warned me not to go back to *Lessen Your Expression*. She said *Raise That Brow Now* was a far superior salon with medically qualified clinicians. I should have stayed with them. Damn my impatience. If I'd waited longer, I would have seen the positive effects of my first session, but I moved on too hastily in search of more instant results. That would be something else I could work on—being a more patient human being. I would scrap my *Little White Lies* notebook in favour of a *How to Become a Better Human Being* notebook.

Speaking of that, I'd better set right the wrong I had committed recently. I had about 40k left of the 50k I'd extorted from Seán. Hmmm, there was no way I was giving it back. That would involve contacting him and talking to him and transferring money. No, I needed to find another avenue. He definitely wouldn't engage with me or trust me, I imagined. Hmmmm, what to do, what to do …

I searched the web for worthy charities to donate to. That way I'd have proof that I was a generous, decent human being and could record it in my notebook. Declan might soften towards me if he discovered that I'd thought of others and done the right thing. I'd somehow let Seán know too, so he'd find out his hard-earned GP money was actually helping someone in need, rather than funding my impossible quest for eternal youth. *It's a win for everyone.* Let's see... I just needed to find the right cause ...

I spent most of my day off doing this and rested a little in the afternoon, following my turbulent night. When Declan arrived home with Lucy, we looked each other in the eye meaningfully, but said nothing. We let Lucy distract us with stories of school. Later, Declan disclosed to me that there'd been an offer made for the house next door. There were two bidders interested and both kept increasing their bids. It was looking as if the house would sell for more than we thought. The latest offer was already 30k above the asking price.

'That's great news, Declan,' I acknowledged, but said no more on the subject. I didn't want him to think I was assuming ownership of the money. Bernadette left the house in his name and I wasn't sure if he was going to share any of it with me. I changed the subject and informed him of the mercy work I'd been doing that day. I was about to tell him what charity I'd picked and how generous I'd been, but Jim rang for a chat and I didn't see him for the rest of the evening.

✧　✧　✧

THANKFULLY, THE FACIAL tenderness had lifted and I was able to apply makeup on the morning I was due in for work. I stopped en route to pop the letter I'd written to Seán in the postbox. I could just imagine his reaction on reading it. He'd be impressed to discover I'd become a philanthropist and was putting his hard-earned cash to good use. I wondered if he'd even send me a thank you note. He knew where I worked and he had my address on file. If he does, I'll stick it into my *How to Be a Better Human Being* notebook. *It will have pride of place in there.* As I walked into the office building, I reminded myself of my words to dear Seán. I hoped I hadn't been overly sentimental, but concluded that it was just the type of person I was naturally morphing into.

Dearest Seán,

Yes, it's been a while, hasn't it? You're probably wondering how I'm getting on, aren't you? Very well in fact, thank you for your concern, my dear Seán.

I thought you would like to know that your money has gone to a wonderful cause! I never had any intention of keeping it. I wouldn't do that, being the kind, generous soul that I am, as well you know. Please find enclosed a receipt for your/our/my charitable donation on your/our/my behalf. Yes, Seán, as a devoted mother, faithful wife and committed HR manager, I feel it is my duty to spread my wings and work for the greater good, or the good of the greatest, whichever way you look at it.

I trust that you are still saving lives by the minute and I want to thank you for your dedication to healthcare. You have played a part in making me the wonderful human being that I now am and I'd like to take this opportunity to thank you and your parents, George and May, for that.

Yours sincerely,
Cara, 'finally letting the light in' Cawley.

Receipt of Payment

Many thanks, Mrs Cara Cawley, for your kind donation of €30,000 to Victims Of Botched Cosmetic Surgery Ireland. This money will be used to fund procedures for women who mistakenly had work done by practitioners who were not registered with the Medical Council of Ireland. This is the most generous donation we have received from a member of the public to date and we would like to erect a plaque in your honour.

Please visit our offices in Merchant's Quay,
City Centre to view your homage.

Oh, I'd love to be a fly on the wall when dear
old Seánie opens his letter. I pushed thoughts of
my precarious position as wife to Declan to the
back of my mind and forced myself to focus on
trying to become a better version of myself. Even
at work, if that was possible! I knew if I could
accomplish some personal improvement, I'd have a
better chance of holding onto Declan. It would
have a knock-on effect, or at least, that's what I
hoped. Soon Declan would realise that I was a
formidable, reasonable human being, although not
quite perfect. And hopefully that would be enough
for him to stay.

Chapter Twenty Four

THERE WAS A spring in my step as I burst through the doors of Crawford's Recruitment Agency.

I was greeted by Kate. 'Hi Cara, feeling better? Oh my, you're wearing lots of makeup today! Are you going out later?'

'What a great idea, Kate! Maybe I will! Maybe we all will! I'll check the social funds in the kitty. Thanks for the compliment. Yes, I look great and feel great too! Abundant blessings upon you, Kate!'

She looked extremely confused, but I supposed she'd need time to get used to me being an absolutely wonderful, faultless human being henceforth.

Moments later, I witnessed Barbara exiting Dr Linda's door. She looked pale as a ghost and completely shook. I sighed. Could I find it in me? Would I go there? I consulted my notebook and repeated a mantra or two from it, in my head of course.

You can have anything you want if you give up the belief that you can't have it.

You didn't come this far to only come this far.

I focussed on those two all morning to build up my compassion. I really wished I'd written down shorter, catchier mantras that rolled off the tongue. These two were giving me a headache with their wordiness. I kept forgetting them and mixing them up. Half the time I was chanting, *You can have anything you want if you've only come this far,* and *You didn't come this far to give up the belief that you can't have it.* Oh, I didn't even know what it meant anymore. It all got lost in translation and muddled up in my brain. Surely, positivity wasn't meant to be this complicated and annoying. It was so new to me and up to now I was struggling to see its relevance.

However, I did look over at Barbara a few times and on each occasion I shivered at how pale, unhealthy and even sad she looked. I thought of Declan and how much I wanted to impress him (and not lose him), so I puffed myself up to be that 'bigger person'. I approached Barbara's desk around lunchtime. She jumped. She actually jumped on her seat in fright.

'Hi Cara, I'm nearly finished with those reports. I had an appointment with Linda, so that set me back a bit. I'll have them on your desk by five, I promise.'

'Barbara, Babs …'

'Babs?'

'Yes, Babs. What is wrong with you? Why are you attending Linda's clinic? And why have you allowed yourself to become demoted, when you've been gunning for the S.A.O job for years now? What happened, Babs?'

'Em, well, you've never called me Babs before. In fact, nobody does.'

'Well, I think it's about time we do. It's friendlier, more personal. Know what I mean?'

She looked perplexed.

'Babs, come with me. Walk with me. We'll go for lunch.'

'Oh Cara, if I'm to finish these reports by five, I really better get on with it. I'll grab some biscuits and a coffee for lunch later. I'll be fine.'

'Barbara! Babs! You're not fine. You look like a ghost. There's something wrong and I … Well, perhaps I can help. You know I've had my own struggles lately and I've come out the other side. Stronger now, as you can see. How about I share some of my newfound wisdom with you? What say you, Babs?'

'What say me? Em, I should really get these reports underway and …'

'Nonsense! Kate can help you with those. Come with, now!' My attempt at kindness ended up sounding somewhat military, like commanding orders from a sergeant major. I registered Barbara's terror. I suppose my friendly enthusiasm frightened people because they weren't used to it, but that would change—Now that I had changed. I vowed that my resting bitch face, for which I was known, would transform into a resting beam face. I made a mental note to add that into my notebook later.

✧   ✧   ✧

I LISTENED TO talk radio to pass the time on the drive home following my first day back. When a new contributor to *The Health Slot* was introduced I nearly crashed the car. Doctor Seán's once familiar and reassuring voice boomed from the speakers. I wondered if his dulcet tones would stir fuzzy feelings in my loins and reignite any quenched flames within. I slowed down to focus on his words.

However, the topic was genital herpes and he spoke in great detail about the symptomatic red bumps that can swell and crust over. He didn't inspire any fuzzy flutters in any part of my body and when he launched into descriptions of painful blisters around the groin, I changed the channel. I couldn't listen anymore and shook my head in pity. *Lord, he must be desperate to earn an extra buck if he's on the national airwaves expounding stuff like this. Oh, how the mighty have fallen.* That said, he has the makings of a celebrity doctor. Maybe this is his foot in the door to the world of media and the nation would soon be seeing him on TV.

For the rest of the journey I reassured myself that he'd need quite a bit of cheering up after getting through that radio slot. I imagined my letter might be sitting in his postbox when he arrived home. Surely the light in my words would give him some welcome respite from talk of sexually transmitted diseases and the like. It might take his mind off all that medical stuff and soothe his nerves. It was my gift to him. And of course, more notebook fodder for me.

✧ ✧ ✧

SUBSEQUENTLY THAT EVENING, I shared with Declan how I'd offered the hand of friendship to Barbara and we'd finally made peace with one another.

'Cancer, you say? The poor thing. That's heartbreaking for her and her family.'

'Yes, I had no idea she was going through any of this. She suffered in silence, because we were all so focussed on our work. She didn't want sympathy. I suppose I just always thought she was completely career driven and nothing could knock her down.'

'I imagine it has taken its toll on her mentally. Is that why she stepped down as boss?'

'Yes, she said Linda advised her to step back a bit to alleviate her stress levels. She wants to go on this medical trial for new chemo drugs, so that's why she's still working. It costs a fortune, apparently.'

'Ah, you never know. You never know what some people are going through, do you?'

'I suppose not. The rumours going around the office about her are brutal, though. There are stories about her husband having affairs, her having an eating disorder and even threats of her children being put into care because she hardly spends any time with them. People are just trying to find a reason why she's lost weight and looks so haggard and tired. I'll have to put a stop to it. It's not right. I think I'll get some advice from Linda on how to handle it.'

'Wow! I never thought I'd see the day when you were trying to do something nice for Barbara. She's always been your nemesis at the office, hasn't she?'

'She has, but I suppose people change. I mean, look at me and how far I've come.' I clocked Declan rubbing his chin, looking dubious. Maybe he didn't have as much faith in my newfound benevolence as I had. I continued regardless. 'I shared with her a little about my mental break-down and our financial difficulties in the past, what with our failed IVF attempts and the cost of it.'

'Oh? And what did she say?'

'She apologised. She actually apologised for never taking the time to chat things over with me and be a listening ear, like I was for her today.'

'Wow! That was big of her, wasn't it?'

'Yes, I suppose it was unexpected, considering her character.'

'Is there something niggling at you?'

'Well, it's just she didn't apologise for nicknam-ing me the RBF in the office. It was more of a general apology.'

'What does that stand for again?'

'Resting bitch face.'

'Oh yes, of course. Maybe she forgot. Sounds like she has a lot going on.'

'Hmmm, I suppose. I thought it at least de-served a mention, but I'll give her time.'

'Well, Cara, I'm proud of you! It seems you really are trying to turn over a new leaf with your kindness to Barbara and giving Seán's money to charity. By the way, I thought you said you'd spent the 10k already. So, how could you give it to charity if you'd already spent it?'

'Declan, I have a perfectly reasonable explana-tion for how I did that. I just need to go and consult my notebook for a few minutes and then I'll share it with you, okay?'

He looked puzzled, as I excused myself and dashed upstairs.

✧   ✧   ✧

TO BE, OR not to be, completely honest with my husband? Hmmm. I needed to think this one out. I hadn't actually gotten rid of my *Little White Lies* notebook yet, so I picked it up and flicked through it. I had made notes of small, insignificant lies I'd told to various people, but they all added up. The notebook was almost full at this stage. It was a great way of keeping track of who I told what and what I told who, and when.

I flicked back to the first page, where I'd transcribed a quote from my dear departed mother. '*Always tell a lie when the truth doesn't fit in.*' Hmmm, I had done that for so long and it didn't serve me. I'd always trusted that my mother knew best. Never doubted her, but now, as a mother and wife myself, I realised that it's probably not the best advice to give and definitely not the best advice to live by. With a heavy heart, I scribbled it out and wrote underneath, '*Honesty is the best Policy.*'

That gave me courage to break the news to Declan. I went back downstairs and joined him on the chesterfield.

'You're right. I did indeed spend the 10k.'

'So, what funds did you use to give to charity?'

'It's just, well, I wasn't entirely honest with you at the time. You see, Seán's pay off was a little more than 10k.'

'Was it? Why did you lie to me about it?'

'Em, I thought I'd use it to surprise you and pay off some debts.'

'You didn't, though. We still owe huge amounts.'

'I did, Declan. I guess this might be another "surprise", but not exactly a good one. I had actually clocked up some extra debts that I hid from you, and I managed to pay them off. But I promise, no more secrecy from now on. No more lies. You have my word.'

He sighed. A heavy sigh. 'Will these revelations ever end, will they? And it's never good news. It's always stuff you've done behind my back without consulting me. You don't respect me, Cara.'

'Declan, you said it yourself. I've turned over a new leaf. I'm a changed woman. I had an epiphany in Rosslare. I love you, Declan. You and Lucy. And I want to focus all my energy into making us the happiest family that we can be.'

'How much?'

'What? How much hidden debt, you mean?'

'No. How much did Seán pay you?'

'Oh. Ffff … em, ffff …'

He waited. I rubbed my furrowed brow, while calculating the sums.

'Forty grand.'

'What? He paid you that much? Did you threaten him? What kind of blackmail tactics did you use? Bloody hell! He must have been scared out of his wits to pay you that much.'

'Well, in fairness, he did do wrong by me. But it's okay. I've forgiven him and I'm expecting a thank you note from him any day now, when he reads about my philanthropy.'

'I doubt that. I doubt you'll ever hear from him again. He must be glad to see the back of you if he paid you that much. How much did you give to charity?'

'T … t … em.' Oh, maths wasn't exactly my strong point. I've always been more of a people person. I needed the *Little White Lies* notebook to work out the numbers.

'Em, th … thir … no, twenty grand. Yes, twenty grand. So, I used 10k to pay off my secret debts, I spent 10k, as you know, on our family holiday and a little cosmetic work. And, yes, that leaves 20k for my charitable donation, doesn't it?'

'Hmm, yes, well I suppose that's a pretty generous amount to give to charity. Which one did you choose in the end?'

Silence.

'Cara? Are you still with me? I asked which charity you went with?'

I looked heavenward and wondered if my dear departed mother was looking down on me now and what advice she'd give me in this particularly sticky predicament I found myself in. I know what she'd say, '*Always tell a lie when the truth doesn't fit in*'. Oh Mother, you knew best, you did. I closed my eyes and apologised to her in my head. I told her I should never have doubted her. I vowed to rewrite her words of wisdom into my new notebook. Her motto would still feature in my *How to Become A Better Human Being* notebook.

'Cara, are you listening to me? Which charity did you donate Doctor Seán's money to?'

I really didn't want my husband to leave me. I needed him. More than I'd ever cared to admit. I loved him and deep down, somewhere in the pit of his heart, he would find enough love to accept me and stay with me. With midlife enlightenment comes great wisdom. I braced myself in anticipation for what would probably be my last ever little white lie. I deemed it a perfectly reasonable one, given the circumstances. I held my breath and swallowed.

'The GAA.'

Chapter Twenty Five

OH BOY, WAS I in Declan's good books after that! He sang my praises to all and sundry at the club. We kept getting invited to this party and that, but could barely go to any due to work commitments. Of course, we also felt the added pressure of finalising the sale of two properties. It was overwhelming, but we vowed to return to Lanzarote for another family holiday as soon as the money from the sales finally arrived in our, well, Declan's account.

In all seriousness, I was humbled that he was willing to extend an olive branch. He hadn't explicitly told me in words, but his actions implied that we were giving our much neglected, floundering marriage a second chance. A few days after the charity donation disclosure, he arrived home with flowers. I didn't admonish him, but rather accepted them gratefully. I cooked him sausages for supper and he beckoned me over to the chesterfield. Without saying anything, he found *GAA Giants* and pressed play.

After ten minutes of watching, and with silence from me, he began explaining who Micky O'Halloran was and what team he played for. He also very kindly shared with me some of the injuries he'd sustained during play in various matches between 2010 and 2013. I replied with exaggerated 'oohhs' and 'aahhs', opening my eyes wider on occasion to look interested.

I didn't raise my brow, for fear of inciting wrinkles. I didn't furrow it either for the same reason. I would be using my eyes from now on for expression, although I was starting to notice a marked increase in deepening crow's feet. Something else to keep a close eye on. Turning forty came with much added responsibility.

Anyway, to cut a long story short, I got through an hour of *GAA Giants* without any complaints. It was very peaceful. I didn't mention how boring I thought it was. I exercised patience and kept it all in.

✧　✧　✧

My husband was so chuffed with my choice of charity that I could now do no wrong in his eyes. I could never admit to him that it was a little white lie I felt compelled to tell, given the immense pressure I was under at the time—it was the way I was raised. But no, he must never know that. I did donate the money to charity anyway. It's not like I kept it for personal use.

I justified the white lie by telling myself that the worthy charity I'd chosen was actually benefiting from an extra 10k than I'd disclosed to my husband. I was, in fact, better and even more genuinely decent than what he was giving me credit for. I really hadn't done anything wrong. And, it was more than likely that the beneficiaries, the poor creatures with botched cosmetic jobs, probably had sons or daughters or husbands who played GAA. Therefore, the money was ultimately ending up in the same place, in a somewhat convoluted, roundabout way.

I firmly believed that anyway, especially when the plaque was erected on the walls of the offices of *Victims Of Botched Cosmetic Surgery Ireland*. I was so deeply proud of myself when I went to be photographed with the CEO of the charity herself. A plaque and a framed photo of me was hung on their walls. This was indeed philanthropy at its finest. My notebook would love this. I stuck in a miniature photo of me holding the plaque, beaming ear to ear, and not a crease in sight on my forehead, which only added to my pride.

In the end, I'd reaped the rewards of two different Botox clinics, albeit through an arduous process, to finally see the end result. My brow wasn't furrowing much now and there was a marked decrease in the number of lines on my forehead. I know this because I counted them regularly. I was pretty sure most women of my age did that.

And, perfectly reasonable it was too.

BEING IN THE good books with my husband afforded me the luxury of being thrown a surprise 40th birthday bash. When the 'dreaded day' finally arrived, I found I wasn't so much dreading it as looking forward to it. I knew Declan had organised something when he informed me to dress up in my finery and 'be ready'. No problem to me. I wore a silk blue wrap dress which hugged my slender figure. My shapely legs were elongated with designer Saint Laurent high-heeled sandals. I looked phenomenal. Both Lucy and Declan told me, but I knew I did anyway. I bought Lucy a long, pink flowergirl's dress from Monsoon with a delicate floral garland hairband. She looked like a sweet little angel.

Declan didn't let me down. He caught me looking out the window at the crowds of neighbours gathering close to our house. He grabbed my waist and pulled me away. 'No, no, a surprise, remember? No peeking!' I laughed excitedly and pecked him on the cheek. His phone beeped and he ordered me and Lucy to make our way downstairs and open the front door.

We couldn't believe the vision that awaited us. A horse and carriage at the foot of the driveway! 'Like a fairytale!' I exclaimed, and Lucy rushed out to pet the white horse. The neighbours clapped for us as we made our way towards the carriage. I looked back as Declan sauntered out shyly with his head down, in the white suit I'd bought for him. He'd looked horrified initially when I showed it to him, claiming it would make him look like Johnny Logan at the Eurovision, but acquiesced in the end. As he put it—"Anything for a quiet life."

He clambered up onto the carriage to join his girls. He caught my smiling eyes as he stepped on board. The three of us sat there like royalty waving at the neighbours. The horse remained stagnant as he relieved himself right outside our driveway. I didn't care. I knew Declan would clean it up in the morning. It gave me a chance to acknowledge the obvious admiration my neighbours were bestowing upon us. I caught Peggy's eye in number 23 as she nodded in approval. I could practically hear her deep, dependable voice telling Mary in number 21 how awestruck she was by the spectacle before her. I imagined it went something like—

'Ahh Mary, would you look! Off they go in their horse and carriage!'

'Ah, there they go, a lovely family, aren't they,

Peggy? Never a peep outta them. And little Lucy up there in the upper class creche. Sure, that's where all the celebrities send their children, you know, Peggy?'

'Oh, indeed I know. It costs an arm and a leg, but I suppose they can afford it, what with Bernadette leaving them her house in her will.'

'Ah, God rest dear Bernadette. Weren't they so good to her after Roger passed away? They took her under their wing. I used to see Declan in and out of her house nearly every day, you know. Mostly late in the evenings, but I suppose he waited until after little Lucy went to bed. Such a kind, family man.'

'Oh yes, what wonderful neighbours. Just a lovely, lovely family and never a moment's trouble outta them.'

'Oh, indeed. They're a genuine, decent, salt of the earth family. They really are!'

I squirmed in delight as I waved royally to dear old Peggy and Mary. It felt good to have impressed the local neighbourhood gossips. I could sense their reverence as they eagerly waved back and gestured their approval, while mouthing words, which seemed to me like, '*only gorgeous*' and '*fabulous*'. My transformation had worked. I was now a well-respected member of the community! Much deserved, I thought to myself, much deserved.

When the carriage driver finished wiping the horse's behind, we set off amid waves and cheers. 'Happy birthday, Cara! You don't look it!' Betty hollered from her doorstep at number 22.

Declan reaffirmed Betty's good wishes. 'You don't look forty at all, Cara! You look radiant, like a princess! My two girls do!' On hearing that, Lucy climbed up on his lap.

'So, Declan, you can tell me now. What's the surprise? Where are we going?' He still hadn't told me where we were off to.

'Cara, remember the good old days, before you went nuts dancing around the kitchen in your knickers?'

'Em, well, yes I suppose I do. What are you getting at?'

'Like the period before you got addicted to the pills that used to make you howl like a lunatic in the night?' He covered Lucy's ears when he said that.

'Em, yes, I can remember, although "addicted" is too strong a word. I rather refer to it as my fleeting flirtation with sleep assistance aids. It sounds more delicate and ...'

'Yeah, so, before your midlife crisis?'

'Yes, Declan, there was a "before" time. I'm aware of that!'

'The first one, like before your FIRST midlife crisis, yeah?'

'Did I have more than one? Is that even possible? I had a few episodes, but they were in such quick succession that I'd lump them under the one crisis umbrella.'

'Right, well, if you say so, but that's not the point. Anyway, remember when you used to sit on the couch with a cup of tea and a biscuit and listen to Bublé to relax and have a good time?'

'Yes. On the chesterfield, you mean? With an artisan handmade biscuit made by the finest Irish biscuit producers. Yes, yes I do remember that.'

'Well, I'm bringing you back to that fantastic time in our lives! Three tickets to Michael Bublé! The afternoon concert, suitable for kids! And then dinner and a party in the club afterwards with all our friends at the GAA, Cara! They're over the moon with your recent generous donation, although the cheque hasn't come through yet. What do you say to that? Surprised?' He never looked prouder. Absolutely chuffed with himself, he was.

'Em, what say I? What say I?'

'Hmm, Cara? Are you speaking backwards?'

'No, no I just tend to do that sometimes … when I'm buying time.'

'Oh, so eh, surprised, are you? Like, in a good way?'

'Yes, yes, darling. I am indeed surprised in a perfectly reasonable way,' I reassured him demurely, with my very best resting beam face.

The End

Epilogue

Dear Diary,

It's been 40 days since I started this journal and I haven't looked back. Little did I ever imagine the rewards I would reap from simply allowing myself to be the person I was meant to be. The person I was put on this earth to be is kind, generous, maternal, full of wifey goodness and sincerely humble. I can't believe I've managed to turn over a new leaf, save my marriage, get a promotion, have the happiest daughter in the world AND still maintain my refined, unparalleled sense of taste and style. I am actually in awe of myself at times!

But back to daily operations now. Yes, of course the cheque for the GAA bounced, as I knew it would. However, luckily I had plan B firmly in place before anyone noticed. And by anyone, I mean Declan. I didn't want to be troubling him with the whole fiasco, so I transferred 20K from the sale of the Rosslare bungalow into the GAA account, and sure, no one is the wiser it seems. Not yet anyway.

Good old Bernadette leaving us such a healthy share of her properties. An angel sent from heaven she was, to free us of our debt and allow us to make charitable donations like this.

I stopped writing for a moment and smiled to myself. Now, I had another guardian angel looking down upon me. Good old Bernie would feature prominently in my *How to Become a Better Person* journal. Her selfless acts of generosity would appear side by side with my mother's sage advice. I could feel my RBM face sparkle as I gazed heavenward. *Lord, it's true what I've always thought-Growing older and wiser is a perfectly reasonable way to grow!*

NOTE FROM THE AUTHOR

Many thanks for taking the time to read this book. If you enjoyed it, I'd be very grateful if you would leave a review.

To find out more about future book releases, please join my mailing list here: rachelrafferty.com/newsletter

If you'd like to connect, you can reach me at: rachelraffertybooks@gmail.com

Printed in Great Britain
by Amazon